MARKED FOR REVENGE

MARKED SERIES BOOK 2

ANNA BLAKELY

MARKED FOR REVENGE

Marked Series 2

Anna Blakely

Marked for Revenge

Marked Series 2

First Edition
Copyright © Anna Blakely
All rights reserved.
All cover art and logo Copyright © 2022
Publisher: Saje Publishing, LLC
Cover by: Lori Jackson
Proofreading by: Angie Springs, Kim Ruiz, and Christine Hall

All rights reserved. No part of this book may be reproduced in any form or by any electronic or mechanical means, including information storage and retrieval systems—except in the case of brief quotations embodied in critical articles or reviews—without permission in writing from the author.

This book is a work of fiction. The names, characters, and places portrayed in this book are entirely products of the author's imagination or used fictitiously. Any resemblance to actual events, locales, or persons, living or dead, is entirely coincidental and not intended by the author.

The unauthorized reproduction or distribution of this copyrighted work is illegal. Criminal copyright infringement, including infringement without monetary gain, is investigated by the FBI and is punishable by up to five years in federal prison and a fine of $250,000.00.

If you find any eBooks being sold or shared illegally, please contact the author at anna@annablakelycom.

❦ Created with Vellum

ABOUT THE BOOK

A killer is on the loose, and he won't stop until he makes everyone pay.

Two years ago, Allie Andrews did what she thought was right...and it cost her everything. Now the criminal she helped to put behind bars has escaped, and he's hunting down everyone responsible for his conviction. Alone and afraid, Allie turns to the only man who can keep her safe. But if she's not careful, the sexy special agent may steal the only part of herself she has left to give—her heart.

FBI Special Agent Wade Crenshaw's need for justice put Allie Andrews in a killer's crosshairs once before. So when he learns she's in danger again, he puts everything on the line to protect her—including his heart. Because this time is different.

This time, Wade's playing for keeps.

While in hiding, Allie and Wade find themselves in a whirlwind of danger and passion. Just when they think the worst is behind them, Allie vanishes without a trace. In an instant, the hunted becomes the hunter as Wade embarks on a mission to save the woman he loves, and failure is not an option.

He lost Allie once before. He damn sure won't lose her forever.

Marked for Revenge is a twisted tale of love and survival. Get ready for a romantic suspense story that will keep your heart pounding and your toes curling as Wade and Allie fight for their lives...and the love they've only just begun to find.

PROLOGUE

Five years ago...

"Have a good night!"

"You, too." Allison Andrews gave the last customer of the night a quick smile and a half-wave. "Thanks, again!"

Waiting for the older gentleman to leave, she grabbed the key ring from the shelf beneath the cash register and walked around the counter's edge. The long day had her moving slow and wishing she didn't have a week's worth of lesson plans waiting for her when she got home.

Just two more months until summer break.

The thought put a slight pep in her step. Teaching kindergarten was her passion, but unfortunately, passion alone didn't pay the bills. Because education wasn't the most lucrative of careers, Allison spent her weekdays in the classroom, and a few evenings and weekends serving tables at Rick's Diner.

Located in historic Old Town, the small restaurant wasn't as high-end as some of the other eating establishments in Alexandria, but that did nothing to diminish its importance to the neighborhood. With a constant stream of customers, the old-fashioned diner offered locals and tourists alike the classic diner experience.

From the Formica tabletops and red vinyl booths to the checkered tile floor and fully functional juke box, it was one of the more upbeat and laid-back businesses on the strip. It didn't hurt that Rick, the diner's owner, was one of the nicest bosses she'd ever worked for.

"That the last one?" Rick hollered through the kitchen's large open window.

Speak of the devil.

"Yep." Allison started toward the booth where the man had been seated.

Picking up his near-empty mug of coffee, she pulled the rag from her apron and wiped the table down. When she got back to the front counter, she handed Rick the dirty mug and rag before returning the keys to their rightful place.

"The tables are clean, and the floor's been swept and mopped. The only thing left to do is wash that mug and count the drawer."

"I wash and you count?" The silver-haired man gave her a knowing grin.

Allison couldn't help but return his contagious smile. It was well-known amongst the employees that Rick despised anything to do with math and money. In fact, he'd tried more than once to talk her into quitting her teaching job to come work for him as his full-time manager.

But every time he asked, Allison always told him the same thing. That she loved her students far too much to ever consider leaving them.

"You wash, I'll count," she agreed.

Giving her an appreciative nod of his head, Rick disappeared as Allison opened the cash register and pulled out the plastic till.

A few minutes later, the day's revenue was figured, and the register was stocked and ready for the morning. Sliding the tiny silver key into the drawer's lock, Allison grabbed the black money bag from the counter and hollered at Rick through the window.

"You want me to put this in the safe?"

"Just set it on my desk." Rick set the newly washed mug on the drying rack. "I'll get it before I leave."

"You sure? I know the combination, so it's not a problem."

"Actually, I changed it a few days ago." He turned and shrugged. "Just as a precaution."

The statement took her by surprise. Allison had worked at Rick's for over a year, and the combo had never been changed. Not that she could argue with the sweet man's logic.

Just like passwords and pin numbers for other things, it probably wasn't a bad idea to mix things up with the small wall safe occasionally.

"Gotcha." She flashed him a smile. "I'll grab the bathroom trash while I'm back there."

"I can take care of that stuff, Allie. You've been going non-stop all day. Not to mention, this was your day off. Go on home."

Another smile was her only response as she turned and headed down the hall. Yes, she'd been on her feet the whole day, and yes, she should've had today off. But Brittney called in sick last-minute, and it wasn't in Allison's nature to turn down a request for help. Especially when the person asking was Rick.

Passing the restrooms, Allison went into his office and

placed the money on his desk. Her lips twitched as she took in the pristine space. The man was as laid back as they came, except when it came to his personal space.

The small room was always pristine. Everything in its place.

Smiling, she went into the men's restroom and pulled the bag of trash from the large can beneath the paper towel holder mounted on the wall. Tying the clear plastic into a knot, she set it in the hall while she did the same with the trash from the women's restroom next door.

With a bag in both hands, Allison spoke loud enough for Rick to hear as she made her way back to the front. "I know you told me to go, but I was already back there, so I went ahead and grabbed these so you wouldn't have to mess with them."

Her statement was met with silence.

Glancing around, she was surprised when her boss was nowhere to be found.

"Rick?" she called out for him as she entered the diner's small kitchen. Lowering her gaze, she noticed the large trash can by the back door was empty. Its lid leaning against the plastic can.

He's out back.

Setting one of the bags down, Allison used her free hand to open the door leading to the alley, and then propped the metal door open with her hip. She picked the bag up once more before moving a bit awkwardly through the open doorway.

"I went ahead and got these, since I was already back—" Allison started to repeat herself. She stopped abruptly when she spotted Rick at the end of the alley, near the building's two dumpsters.

His back was to her, and he wasn't alone.

Right away, she recognized one of the two men standing with her boss. A tad shorter than Rick, the dark-haired man came into the diner about once every couple of weeks or so, and he was always alone.

He never ordered much. A piece of cherry pie and cup of coffee was his usual go-to. He took his time eating and drinking, keeping to himself as he sat in his booth people-watching. Or at least, that's what Allison always assumed.

Standing tall—about six feet, give or take—the other man with Rick had short, silver hair and black glasses. Allison's memory wasn't perfect, but she hardly ever forgot a face. And his was one she'd never seen before.

"I thought I told you to go home." Rick scowled at her from over his shoulder.

His uncharacteristically gruff tone threw her off guard. Not once in the thirteen months she'd worked for him had he ever spoken to her in that manner.

"I know." Allison forced a smile. "I just wanted to let you know you didn't have to worry about the bathroom trash."

Holding the two bags up for him to see, she walked the few steps separating her from the nearest dumpster. One at a time, Allison tossed the trash inside before closing the metal lid and wiping her hands on the front of her black waist apron.

The two men Rick was talking to both shifted their gazes to her. Their cold, unemotional stares sending an unsettling shiver racing down the length of her spine.

This isn't right. Something's not right.

Ignoring the gnawing feeling in her gut, Allison forced her tone to remain steady as she focused solely on Rick. "Is everything okay, Boss?"

"Yeah." Rick answered a little too quickly. "Of course. These guys are friends of mine. They just happened to be walking by when they saw me and decided to stop and catch up.

Friends?

Allison had met a few of Rick's friends over the past year, and *none* of them created the feeling of unease these two did.

Even so, she had no concrete reason to believe her boss wasn't telling the truth about who his so-called friends were. Just a gut feeling she couldn't explain.

Still, Allison studied the men closely, committing their faces to memory. Just in case.

She flashed her boss another friendly smile. "If you're sure you don't need me to do anything else—"

"I'm good, Allison." Rick tipped his head. "I'll see you tomorrow."

"See you tomorrow."

With that, she turned around and walked back into the diner. Closing the door behind her, she made it a whole five feet before something else struck her as odd.

He called me Allison.

From day one, Rick had always called her Allie. Never Allison.

Spinning on her heels, she went back to the door and turned the knob. Opening it slowly to avoid detection, she cracked it just enough to get a clear view of where Rick and the other men were still standing.

She knew she should probably feel bad for spying, but Rick wasn't just her boss. He was her friend, and if those guys were bad news...

"I'm sorry." Rick's pleading voice reached her ears before she saw him. "Look, forget I said anything, okay? I-I don't know what I was thinking."

The taller man hovered over Rick in an intimidating

stance. "Seems pretty clear to me, Richard. You were thinking you were going to cut my business off at its knees."

His business?

"No. I-I'd never..." Her boss shook his head frantically. "Forget I said anything. We'll keep the operation going the way it always has been."

"Do you remember what I told you at our first meeting?" The tall man crowded into Rick's personal space.

"Th-that was a long time ago, Mr. Costa."

Rick sounded scared. Terrified, even.

"Yes, well, let me refresh your memory." The man her boss had referred to as Mr. Costa straightened his spine. "I told you I don't do business with men I can't trust."

The other man, the shorter one, remained stoically silent.

"You *can* trust me!"

Rick took a step toward Costa but stopped when the shorter man put himself in Rick's path. Raising his hands in front of him, Rick appeared to be showing them he wasn't a threat.

What the hell?

"I wish that were true." Costa took a step backward.

"Wait!" Rick shook his head.

"Goodbye, Richard." Costa turned to leave.

Allison waited, her pulse racing through her veins as she waited for the two men to leave. Whatever Rick had gotten himself into, it sounded bad. Really bad. But from what Costa had just said, his dealings with her boss had come to an end.

"Mr. Costa, please," Rick begged the man walking away.

Allison's gaze shifted to Costa. She watched him closely. Listened intently. But he never said another word.

Instead, the intimidating man turned to the shorter man and gave him a single nod.

What happened next seemed like something out of a dream. Or, in this case...a horrifying nightmare.

Frozen by fear and disbelief, Allison could do nothing but watch as the shorter man pulled a gun from his back waistband and pointed it straight at Rick.

No!

"Wait!" Rick lifted his hands. "Please, Eddie. You don't have to do this."

"You know how this works, Ricky. Gotta do what the boss says."

"I'm begging you." Rick fell to his knees. "I-I have a wife. My daughter's about to give birth to my first grandchild. *Please!*"

"Sorry, Ricky." The man with the gun shrugged. "It's nothin' personal."

"Don't!"

A low zip of a sound cut through the night air. At the same time, Rick's body jerked, the back of his head exploding in a misting spray of blood and tissue.

Dear God, no!

Seconds later, the man Allison had come to care a great deal about was lying dead on the ground. Left in the alley next to the dumpster, as if he were as meaningless as the garbage inside.

"*No!*"

Costa and Eddie stopped suddenly, their eyes locking with hers.

"Get her!" Costa ordered the man who'd just put a bullet through Rick's head.

Oh, God! They heard me! They know I saw what happened. I know what they did.

And unless she got her ass in gear and moved *now*, he was going to kill her, too.

Snapping herself out of the shocked trance, Allison slammed the diner's back door shut and slid the deadbolt and knob locks into place. She started to run to the front door, but stopped so quickly, the soles of her tennis shoes slid across the newly cleaned tile.

The back door was heavy. Industrial in strength. Not impossible to break down, but not as likely as say, a glass door like the one she was headed for.

They'll come through there!

She swung around and stared at the open door at the end of the hall. *Rick's office.*

Her chin quivered, and tears burned the corners of her eyes. But she pushed it all aside and sprinted toward the small room.

A room with a window large enough for her to fit through.

Once she was inside, Allison shut the door as quietly as she could before locking it. A loud banging sound came from somewhere out front. A warning that time was running out.

Heart pounding so hard she felt as though it would fly right out of her chest, she ran to Rick's desk. Using his chair as a stepstool, Allison rolled it back, carefully balancing herself to keep the seat from swiveling as she placed her right foot on the cushion.

Her legs shook so badly, she was certain her knees would give out any second, but somehow Allison managed to pull herself up to the small bookshelf positioned beneath the window. Releasing the lock, she wasted no time in sliding the pane up and hoisting herself over the sill.

Wood and metal pressed painfully against her midsection, but she refused to stop. Angry male voices reached her ears, motivating her to move faster.

Doing her best to remain silent, Allison bit back a grunt as she slid the rest of the way through the window. First one leg, and then the other. Her feet hit the ground below a fraction of a second before her would-be assassins burst through the office door.

"The window!" she heard someone yell.

Shit!

Rising from a crouched position, Allison took off down the narrow space separating the diner and the building to the west. Her leg muscles burned, but she didn't dare slow down.

Not when her left calf started to cramp. Not when her lungs burned with the need to catch her breath. Not even when a bullet meant to end her life zinged past her head.

Releasing a small whimper of a sound, Allison pushed herself harder. Moved faster. Until she found herself in the middle of the street, horns blaring as cars swerved to miss her.

Tires squealed, their rubber burning across the dark pavement. She jumped, screaming as the palms of her hands slapped down onto the hood of a car that nearly ran her down.

It took her two full seconds to realize the vehicle that had nearly struck her was Alexandria P.D.

"Oh, thank God!" she cried as the officer exited his vehicle.

The young man rushed to her side. "Are you okay?"

I just saw my boss get shot in the head. Hell no, I'm not okay!

Allison shook her head, tears falling freely down her cheeks as she pointed back down the alley. "They killed him!" She drew in a stuttered breath. "Th-they shot him in cold blood, and then they left him there as if he were nothing. And n-now they're trying to k-kill me, t-too!"

She knew she sounded hysterical, but she didn't care. The more attention she drew, the better her chances that someone would listen to her.

"Whoa. Easy, there."

"Please. My b-boss!" Her face began to crumble, but Allison forced herself to regain her composure. "He's back there, all alone."

The policeman needed to understand. She wasn't some crazed lunatic who enjoyed running into heavy traffic, but rather the sole witness to a gruesome murder.

"Okay." He attempted to calm her down. "Listen, I'm going to help you. But let's get you out of the road and over to the sidewalk where it's safe."

With a shaky nod, Allison walked woodenly as the kind officer guided her out of the street.

Pulling out a small notebook and pen from his crisply pressed uniform shirt, he said, "Let's start with your name."

"A-Allison Andrews."

"Okay, Allison. I'm Officer Nichols. Why don't you start from the beginning?" The young man's brow furrowed. "Now, did you say someone's been *killed*?"

Even in her scattered state of mind, Allison understood the officer's confusion. The overall crime rate in Alexandria was much lower than the national average. It was one of the reasons her parents had chosen to move here nearly twenty-nine years ago, a few short months before she was born.

"My boss, Richard Easton." It was a miracle she could utter his name without completely breaking down. "H-he owns Rick's Diner right over there." Allison pointed at the building behind her. "I was taking out the trash and saw him talking to two men in the alley out back. I went back inside, but something felt off, so I opened the door again, just enough to be able to see and hear them."

"When you say 'off', what do you mean?"

"They gave me the creeps. The way they spoke to Rick… it was obvious he was in some kind of trouble with them."

"What kind of trouble?"

"I-I don't know." Allison ran a hand through her hair. "But whatever it was, they killed him for it."

Making a few more notes, he closed the notebook and offered her a kind smile. "Okay, Miss Andrews. I'm going to call this in so we can get some more units out here to check out the scene. Would you feel better if you waited in my car while I do that?"

"Yes, please." She was quick to take him up on the offer. Being out in the open like this made her feel far too vulnerable.

"Not a problem. First, I'll need to pat you down for my safety and yours. If you're not comfortable with that, we can wait for a female officer to—"

"It's fine." Allison lifted her trembling arms to her sides and straightened her shoulders. "Do whatever you need to do."

After a quick and respectful pat down, she found herself sitting in the front passenger seat of Officer Nichols' squad car. The smell of leather filled the enclosed space as she stared out the window, her eyes locked on the cop standing a few feet away.

Before long, the entire block was a sea of flashing lights and yellow tape. Police and other first responders moved about with purpose, preserving the gruesome scene while controlling the growing crowd.

It was like something out of a movie.

What felt like hours later, Allison was still sitting there, watching it all through the windshield when a dark, imposing figure came into view. She jumped when whoever it was knocked on the passenger window.

Spotting the shiny gold badge attached to the man's belt, she felt it was safe to roll the window down.

"Miss Andrews?" The man leaned down so she could see his face. "I'm Special Agent Wade Crenshaw with the FBI. Would you mind stepping out of the vehicle? I'd like to ask you a few questions."

FBI?

Allison looked around at the other nearby officers before returning her gaze to the man beside the car. Sensing her hesitation, the handsome agent unfolded his leather ID holder and held it up so she could verify the claim.

Trusting that the ID was real, Allison pulled on the door's handle and pushed it open. She was surprised at the steadiness in her legs when she slid out of the car and rose to her feet.

Standing next to him, she could see that he was tall. Much taller than her petite, five-three frame. A set of broad shoulders filled the shoulders of his navy blue blazer. muscular chest stretched the white button-down he had tucked into a pair of dark pants, and a black tie and navy blue windbreaker with yellow lettering finished off his stereotypical FBI persona.

"I know you've had a rough night, so I'll try to make this quick," he rasped.

Handsome and thoughtful.

The thought nearly had her physically recoiling. Those were things she absolutely should *not* be noticing right now.

Putting the inappropriate thought out of her mind, Allison hugged herself as she fought a chill that had nothing to do with the weather. "Thanks. I appreciate that."

The agent's dark gaze seemed to blanket her with a sense of warmth and safety. But then he blinked, clearing his throat as he pulled a black leather-padded notebook from his right jacket pocket.

"So, you work at Rick's Diner?" He studied his notes.

"Only part-time. I also teach Kindergarten over at John Adams Elementary."

"Okay." The corner of his lips threatened to lift. "Now, you told Officer Nichols you saw the men responsible for your boss's death. Can you describe them for me? And take your time. Sometimes even the smallest of details can make all the difference."

She didn't need to take her time. The faces of the men she saw tonight would haunt her for the rest of her life.

"One was shorter," she told him. "About five-ten or so. He had black hair, wore a black leather jacket and jeans. Rick..." Allison's voice cracked, causing her to clear her throat in order to continue. "Rick called him Eddie."

"Good." Agent Crenshaw nodded as he wrote the description in his own tiny notebook. "That's really good. What can you tell me about the other man?"

"He was taller, around six feet, maybe? And older. I'd guess in his mid-fifties, maybe early sixties." The man's cold stare would be forever engrained in her memory. "Oh, and Rick said his name. Mr. Costa."

The sexy agent's hand froze, his intense gaze flying up to hers. "You're *sure* that's the name Mr. Easton used?"

"I'm positive." She hugged herself a little tighter. "Rick never said his first name, but I'm one hundred percent sure Costa was the man's last name. Why?"

Rather than answer her, Agent Crenshaw pulled out his phone and began swiping at the screen. Stopping suddenly, he held the device up for her to see.

"Is this the man you saw in the alley with your boss?"

It took Allison all of two seconds to be sure. "That's him." She nodded. "That's the man who gave the order for Rick to be killed."

Excitement she didn't understand flashed behind the agent's eyes. "Miss Andrews—"

"Allison," she corrected him. "Some people call me Allie."

"Okay, Allie." He smiled. "Listen, I'm going to need you to come with me."

"What? Why? I've already told you and the other officer everything that happened."

"I understand your frustration, but the man you just identified? His name is Lorenzo Costa."

Searching through her memories, Allison frowned. "Should I know who that is?"

"Lorenzo Costa is the head of the largest Italian organized crime syndicate on the east coast." He slid his fingertip across the phone's slick screen and held it up once more. "And Eddie Veneto is his hitman."

Allison could feel the blood draining from her face. Nausea filled her stomach, and she had to swallow several times to keep from throwing up.

Organized crime? Hitman?

Oh, Rick. What the hell did you get yourself into?

"Allie?" Agent Crenshaw's brows bunched together. "I need to know. Is this the other man you saw with your boss?"

"Y-yeah." She gave him a shaky nod. "That's him. He's the one who shot Rick. And before you ask, yes." Allison lifted her gaze to his. "I'm sure."

The man's lips twitched as if he were fighting a smile before he cleared his throat and slid the phone into his back pocket. "Would you be willing to testify in court to what you saw and heard?"

"You want me to testify against a known mob boss and his gun for hire?"

"We can keep you safe," he vowed. "We'll take you someplace where you'll have twenty-four-hour protection, and—"

"Wait a minute." Allison held up a hand to stop him. "You want to put me into protective custody?" She ran a hand over the top of her head, her mind whirling. "This can't be happening." How the hell could this be happening?

"It would just be until the trial is over."

"That could take months, Agent Crenshaw." Years, even.

At least that's how it always seemed to work in the movies.

With his hands resting low on his narrow hips, he stared down at her with understanding...and determination. "Look, I get that the situation isn't ideal, but—"

"Not ideal?" Allison laughed humorlessly. "I just watched my boss...my *friend*...get his brains blown out. And then, I had to climb out a freaking window and nearly got hit by a car because the men who killed him were trying to kill me, too. So yeah, Agent Crenshaw." She crossed her arms in front of her. "I'd say the situation is far from *ideal*."

Hearing her elevated voice, several nearby police officers stopped what they were doing and stared.

Okay, so maybe yelling at a federal agent wasn't the wisest of choices. But after nearly dying at the hands of a mafia kingpin, Allison wasn't exactly feeling like her usually calm self.

"You're right." The man standing before her blew out a breath. "I'm sorry. I didn't mean to make light of what's happened here tonight. But Allie...the Bureau's been after

Costa and his men for years. Murder, drugs, money laundering, sex trafficking...you name it, he does it. We know this, yet every time we think we're getting close to nailing the bastard, he either disappears or gets off on some sort of technicality."

She was shaking her head before he even finished making his case. "I can't just pack up and leave everything behind. I have a job. And my parents—"

"Will also be protected." He took a step toward her. "Come on, Allison. This guy's been virtually untouchable for years. We haven't been able to make a single charge stick, but with your testimony, we can finally put the bastard away for good."

Allison wanted to be brave. She wanted to throw her shoulders back and tell the heartthrob of an agent that she was willing to risk her life—her parents' lives—in order to make the man responsible for Rick's death pay.

But she wasn't brave. She was terrified. And as much as she wanted to be the strong woman she'd always *thought* she was, Allison couldn't find enough inner strength to step up and do what needed to be done.

"I'm sorry." Her eyes rose to meet his. "I wish I could help, but I—"

Movement to her left caught her eye. Turning toward it, Allison's heart shattered all over again when she saw two men pushing a gurney carrying what she assumed was Rick's covered body.

Her vision blurred as they loaded him in the back of the coroner's black van, her muscles tensing when they slammed the doors shut. A life cut short at the hands of senseless violence.

Violence that would no doubt continue if they didn't catch the bastards responsible.

"Rick was a good man," she muttered low. "He wouldn't have gotten involved with someone like Costa unless he felt he had no choice."

"There's always a choice, Allie." Shoving his hands into his pockets, Agent Crenshaw followed her gaze. "For all of us."

The truth of that statement was like a sucker punch to the gut. Mainly because he was right.

As the van carrying her friend vanished into the night, Allison realized what she had to do.

I'll make them pay for what they did to you, Rick. If it's the last thing I do.

"I'll do it." Allison wiped her eyes dry and turned her attention back to the only man who could help her do what needed to be done. "I'll testify against Costa and Veneto."

"Thank you." Relief filtered through Agent Crenshaw's pewter stare as his lips curved into a wide smile. "I promise, you won't regret it."

As she followed him to his government-issued car, Allison couldn't help but wonder if it was a promise he'd be able to keep.

1

Present Day...

A flash of pain registered in Wade Crenshaw's jaw. No stranger to hand-to-hand combat, he struck back, hitting his opponent with a swift uppercut to the chin.

The move shot the guy right off his feet.

Landing with a hollow thud, the other man lay on his back with his eyes squeezed shut. Groaning, he rolled to his side with the intent of standing, but when Wade noticed the guy's struggle, he took a step forward.

Bending at his waist, he reached out toward the man, and then he...offered the guy his hand.

Noah Killion slapped his palm against Wade's, using their combined grip to pull himself to his feet. Rubbing his hand along his jaw, the senior FBI agent's dark eyes met his.

"Thanks."

"Sorry about that," Wade offered his partner a mumbled apology. He hadn't meant to hit the guy so hard.

"All good." Noah rubbed the side of his jaw. "But you'd

better hope that doesn't leave a bruise. Otherwise, Maggie might demand a rematch."

"Name the time and place, brother," Wade joked.

"Wasn't talking about with me. I meant with *her*."

At that, Wade released a low chuckle. "Like I'd fight your wife in the ring."

Just the idea turned his gut.

He and Noah were in the business of protecting the innocent and taking down the bad guys. There wasn't a man in their unit who would *ever* lay a hand on a woman in anger.

Not fucking ever.

"Hey, don't underestimate Mags." A sparkle of admiration for his new wife brightened Noah's gaze as he began to unwrap the tape from his knuckles. "She might be small, but she's a lot tougher than she looks."

"Oh, I remember."

The teasing quip was meant in jest, but Wade was slammed with a hefty dose of guilt when a shadow of pain darkened his friend's expression. Wade knew Noah was remembering just how close he'd come to losing Maggie a few months back.

The two lovebirds first met when Noah flew to Dallas to consult on a case directly related to one of theirs. At the time, Maggie was Dallas's Chief ME, and to hear Noah talk, it was love at first sight.

Several months later, Noah called in a favor, and Maggie came to Denver to help catch a sadistic serial killer that had been terrorizing their city.

At the time, they had no idea the man who'd been abducting and killing women in the Denver area was one of their own. A man Maggie had managed to fight off long enough for Noah to show up and take the bastard out.

In the end, Maggie walked away with a few cuts and bruises, and the killer was put into the ground.

Since then, Maggie had been offered a permanent position as Denver's Chief ME, and she and Noah were now living together in marital bliss.

"Sorry, man," Wade offered. "I didn't mean to bring shit up again."

"Don't worry about it." Noah waved off his apology. "What happened to her will always be there, but she's doing good now. *Really* good. Thanks to you."

He snorted. "My ass was lying in a hospital bed with a hole in my gut. *You're* the one who killed the bastard."

"Only because you identified him as the shooter."

"Fine. We're a couple of badass heroes. Better?"

Pretending to think it over, Noah rubbed the salt and pepper scruff covering his jaw before giving his head a slight nod. "It'll do."

Chuckling, Wade began pulling the tape from his fists and shook his head. And just like that, the tense moment had passed.

"Hey, I forgot to tell you… Maggie has a friend she thinks you should meet. She owns that little coffee shop a couple blocks from here."

"The Roast and Toast?" Wade shook his head. "No thanks."

"Come on, man. You haven't even met the woman."

"I have, actually."

"So what's the problem? From what I've seen, she's cute…seems nice enough. And she owns a successful business, so she's independent and financially stable."

"Yeah, and she has marriage, kids, and the whole picket fence dream written all over her."

Noah's dark brows bunched together. "And what's wrong with that?"

Shit. "Nothing," he rushed to say. "For people like you and Maggie." And the woman they were trying to set him up with. "But that shit's not for me."

Not unless it was with her.

The unexpected thought nearly left him stumbling. Damn it, just when Wade thought he'd finally moved on from that whole pointless, impossible dream, the memories came rushing right back. And it was always when he least expected it.

Like now.

Wanting to put an end to the awkward conversation, he bent down, slid through the ring's ropes, and hopped to the floor below. Noah followed, as did the man's annoying persistence.

"Why not?" Noah pulled the final piece of tape from his own hand as they made their way over to where they'd left their bags. "You won't know if that *shit*, as you called it, is for you unless you actually put yourself out there."

"I'm good, thanks." Tossing his wad of tape into a nearby trashcan, Wade yanked a terrycloth hand towel from his duffle and wiped the sweat from his face and neck.

"Dude, it's been months since you've gone on a date." Noah grabbed his own towel. "If you don't want us to set you up with the coffee shop owner, you could at least try to find someone yourself." Noah tossed the towel aside and slid a t-shirt over his head. "If you're afraid you've lost your mojo, I could give you some pointers. You know, in case you ever decided to actually put yourself out there and go on a... what's that one thing again?" Noah's expression became serious, as if he were deep in thought. A second later, he snapped his fingers and smiled. "Oh, yeah. I think the kids call it a *date*."

"Fuck you," Wade shot back playfully. "I do just fine in that department, thank you very much. For the record, just because I don't announce every time I go out with a woman doesn't mean I *never* do. And I sure as hell don't need any pointers from you or anyone else on that count."

What he didn't say, what he didn't dare admit out loud, was that there was only one woman he was interested in. And she was way the hell out of his reach.

"If you say so." Noah pulled out his water bottle and took a swig.

"I do."

"Good to know."

Shooting his partner a glare that held no real heat, Wade was reaching for his own water when the Breaking News banner on one of the gym's wall-mounted TV's caught his eye. The face filling the screen above the banner had his chest tightening and his heart slamming against his chest.

What the actual fuck?

"Hey, Pauly!" He hollered at the man standing just outside the office door. "Can you turn that up?"

Pauly, the MMA gym's manager, walked over to a small table and picked up a remote. Pointing it toward the TV in question, he turned the volume up high enough for Wade—and everyone else in the gym—to hear.

"Convicted Mafia boss and murderer, Lorenzo Costa, has escaped federal custody this morning after the transport van he and three other inmates were in was ambushed by a group of armed men."

"Oh, shit." Noah turned to him. "Wait...Costa. Wasn't he yours?"

Wade ran a hand over his jaw before replying, his gut

churning as he stared at the screen. "It was the last case I worked before transferring here."

It was also the *reason* he'd requested the move.

"Dash cam footage from the prison van shows a black SUV pulling onto the two-lane highway running west between Red Onion State Prison, Virginia's supermax prison located in Wise County," the anchorman continued. "Authorities believe the SUV was hidden by a thick batch of trees, which made it impossible for the driver of the federal transport van to see it until it was too late. Though the video doesn't show its arrival, a source within DC's FBI headquarters has confirmed there were actually *two* vehicles involved in the ambush, which you will see at the end of the video as both SUVs leave the scene. The sound has been turned off, but I must warn you, the images you are about to see are extremely violent in nature and may be disturbing to some viewers."

"Which is exactly why they're showing it." Noah shook his head in disgust. "The media knows full well that people get off on this shit. That's why they blast it all over the fucking place. They don't care if they upset their viewers or if it's 'disturbing' to watch." The pissed off agent used air quotes. "All they care about is getting a boost in their ratings."

"Shh..." Wade held up a hand to silence his partner.

Noah's assessment was spot-on, but that didn't keep Wade from hanging onto every one of the news anchor's words. He needed to know everything about what had happened. Even if it came from a jackass like the one currently filling the screen.

Standing closer to the TV, both men watched closely as the grainy video began. In it, a dark SUV seemed to appear out of nowhere, skidding to a halt directly in the van's path.

Four men dressed in head-to-toe black jumped out of the SUV, their automatic rifles pointed directly at the driver of the van.

Because the dash camera only showed what was happening in front of the van, it was impossible to see exactly what went down inside, but the minute Costa climbed inside the SUV, the masked men opened fire on the prison van.

"FBI sources have confirmed that all five of the men who remained inside the government vehicle were pronounced dead at the scene, including the driver and a second prison guard. Our prayers go out to the families of the deceased, and we will bring you more information on this story as it unfolds."

The station went back to the program that was already in progress before the breaking news interruption.

Without a word, Wade spun on his heels and rushed back to his bag. Digging past the toiletry bag and change of clothes, he pulled out his phone. Dialing a number he hadn't used in over a year, he put the device to his ear and waited.

"Who you calling?"

"My old partner." The phone continued to ring. "Landry still works at the D.C. office. He'll be able to tell me if they have any leads."

"Uh..not to point out the obvious, but this isn't our case."

Landry's voicemail picked up, prompting Wade to leave a message. Waiting for the beep, he kept it short and sweet.

"Hey, Ryan. It's me. I just saw the news, and I need you to call me as soon as you can." Ending the call, he turned back to his current partner. "No, it's not my case, but it was. For two solid years, Ryan and I busted our asses to find a way to take Costa down."

"I remember hearing about it." Noah nodded. "You two were the talk of every Bureau office across the country for weeks. Bet you got even more attention back in D.C."

"Only Ryan and I weren't the ones to put him away."

"There was a witness, right? Some woman who saw Costa and his strongarm kill a man."

"Allison Andrews." The name felt foreign on his tongue. "She was one of the best eyewitnesses I've ever worked with." And the bravest.

"You think he'll go after her?"

It was a valid question. One that had entered Wade's mind the second he saw the newscast.

"I don't know," he answered honestly. "But I can't take that chance."

Noah studied him with a knowing glance. "You know where she is?"

"No." Something that was always there, gnawing away at him like a slow-growing disease. "She was taken into protective custody prior to the trial. After, the plan was to put her into WITSEC, just until the smoke blew over and we knew the conviction was going to stick. But then her apartment building was torched, and her parents began receiving threats..." Wade raked his fingers through his hair. "The Bureau ended up moving them to an undisclosed location while Allie remained in Witness Protection. Far as I know, she's still living under the new I.D. the Marshals set up for her five years ago."

"Allie?" Noah raised a dark brow.

Shit. "That's what her friends called her."

"And were you?" his partner asked. "Friends, I mean?"

"I was the lead agent on scene the night her boss was murdered. I took her statement, and I..." He swallowed his guilt. "I was the one who convinced her to testify."

"You did your job. And you still didn't answer my question."

"The woman lost everything because of me." Wade scowled. "Her job, her home...her parents. All so I could make a name for myself with the Bureau. So no, we weren't exactly what I'd call friends."

There was a time when Wade thought maybe, just maybe, they could be friends. Possibly more. But that was a lifetime ago, before he'd broken every promise he'd ever made to her.

"Bullshit. I know the kind of agent you are, Wade. The kind of *man* you are. Getting that woman to testify meant getting a career criminal and murderer off the streets. Who knows how many lives you saved by taking Costa down?"

Yeah, that's what he'd told himself back then, too. He was focused solely on the bigger picture. Had convinced himself that one ruined life was a small price to pay for the greater good.

By the time he realized just how wrong he'd been, it was too late.

"Guess it doesn't really matter now, does it?" Wade stormed back over to his bag. "The son of a bitch is back out there. That set up was well-planned, which means it's been in the works for a while."

"Guy's been in a heavily-guarded prison for half a decade. He'll probably find his way to some non-extraditable country where he can enjoy life as a free man."

Shaking his head, Wade slid the strap to his duffle bag over his shoulder and started toward the back of the gym. "That's not Costa's style."

"Okay, fine." Noah grabbed his things and followed. "What do you think his plan is?"

"I don't know, but guys like him? They don't just forgive and forget."

"So, what are you going to do?"

Opening the door to the men's locker room, Wade glanced back at his partner and said, "First, I'm going to shower. Then I'm going to get to work finding that son of a bitch."

Nearly dying had affected him in many ways. Most of all, it opened his eyes to what was missing from the life he'd nearly lost.

Allie.

That was something he intended to rectify as soon as humanly possible, but first, he needed to make sure she was safe. Which meant neutralizing any and all threats against her.

He took Lorenzo Costa down once before. He damn sure would do it again.

2

ALLISON—ALLYSSA Anderson to her fellow Salado, Texas citizens—stared at the TV with horror and disbelief. The man she'd helped to put in prison had escaped, and according to the news, authorities had no idea where he was.

Oh, God.

Pulse racing, she rushed across her apartment's wood floors to her kitchen. Grabbing her purse from where it hung from the back of a bar stool, Allison yanked the burner phone from the inside pocket. She turned it on and called one of two numbers saved in its contact list.

Then she waited.

"Come on, John." Her entire body trembled as she waited. "Please pick up."

Three rings later, the U.S. Marshal assigned to her case answered her call.

"Allyssa." John Napier used the name given to her by the U.S. Marshals five years earlier. "I was about to call you."

"Have you caught him yet?"

"Damn media," the middle-aged man muttered. "That's actually why I was going to call you."

"You didn't answer my question, John. Have you caught him?"

The fifty-five-year-old government agent sighed. "Not yet. But we will."

"How do you know? He could've flown halfway across the country by now! He could be headed *here!*"

Fear had Allison racing to her door to check the locks. As she continued speaking to the man she now only spoke to once a year, Allison moved about her apartment at a near-frantic pace, double-checking that every window in her third-floor apartment was secured.

"Costa won't come for you," John assured her. "One, he has no way of knowing where you are. And two, coming after the sole eyewitness in his murder case right after escaping would only make things worse for him. A move like that would be incredibly stupid, and you and I both know Lorenzo Costa is a lot of things, but stupid isn't one of them."

No, she supposed he wasn't. "What should I do?"

"Nothing."

"Nothing?" Allison scoffed. "The man I saw murder my boss in cold blood just escaped federal custody, and you expect me to do *nothing?*"

"Yes," John stated very matter-of-factly. "I want you to go on living life in that quaint little town of yours, the same way you have for the last five years."

Was he serious? "John, I can't just go to work and come home as if nothing were wrong."

"You have to, Allyssa. I know it's hard, but that's how the program was designed to work. Any deviation from your regular routine could raise suspicion, and that's the last thing we want to do. Especially now. You understand that don't you, Allyssa?"

"My name's not Allyssa, it's Allison!" she yelled.

Something she silently reminded herself on a daily basis for fear she'd wake up one day and forget who she really was.

After a slight pause, John's tone softened as he attempted to talk her down from the proverbial ledge. "Look, I know you're scared, but we've been over this before. Allison Andrews ceased to exist the day you agreed to enter the program. You *are* Allyssa Anderson, now."

"The only reason I agreed to become someone else was because I was told it would be temporary. Five years is a long damn time past that, wouldn't you agree?"

"I understand your frustration, but—"

"Really?" she challenged. "I don't recall you being the one who was ripped from the only life you've ever known. You weren't separated from your family and forced to move to a town full of strangers clear across the country. I don't remember *you* having to change your name and the way you look just so you wouldn't be recognized by anyone who might possibly know you. And you haven't had to spend the last five years pretending to be someone you're not to avoid being gunned down in the street by the freaking mob. So please don't insult me by saying you understand, because you don't."

There was a stretch of silence before she heard John clear his throat.

"Fair enough," he muttered. "You're right, I don't fully understand what you're going through, but I've been at this long enough to understand the frustrations that come with being in WITSEC. All I'm saying is, as of right now, there isn't any evidence to suggest Costa is actively looking for you."

"Of course, there isn't," she snapped back. "It's not like he's gonna leave a detailed map of his plans for the cops to find!"

Allison regretted the snarky outburst the second the words crossed her lips.

Closing her eyes, she drew in a slow, cleansing breath. This wasn't John's fault. None of it was. He just happened to be the unlucky Marshal assigned to her case.

But over the years, John had become more than just her government contact. He was someone Allison considered a friend.

Her only *true* friend, since he was the only one who knew the truth about who she was.

"I'm sorry," she apologized. "I know you mean well. I'm just...."

"Scared," John finished for her. "That's only natural for someone in your position. But listen, I'm going to put a call into Agent Landry. You remember him, don't you?"

"Of course."

She remembered *every* key player involved in the case against Costa. Their names and faces were all burned into the memories of that horrible, awful time in her life.

Ryan Landry was one of two FBI agents responsible for arresting Costa based off her eyewitness statement all those years ago. But he wasn't the lead investigator, which made her wonder...

"Why not Wade, uh, Agent Crenshaw? He was the one in charge of the case. Shouldn't he be the one you—"

"Agent Crenshaw is no longer working out of the D.C. office."

"What?" Allison frowned. "Why not?"

"Wade works out of the Denver division now."

Wade had left D.C.? Why hadn't he gotten in touch with her to let her know?

Probably for the same reason he hasn't bothered to check on you since right after you got here. Wade Crenshaw doesn't care about you. Apparently, he never did.

There was a time when she would've fought that line of thinking, tooth and nail. Back when the sexy FBI agent had watched over her. Protected her.

Kissed her.

But the voice in her head was right. It was all an act, and she'd fallen for it hook, line, and sinker. The only thing that man ever cared about was making his case.

A fact proven by his sudden absence in her life following the guilty verdict.

"I promise, if there's even a *hint* that Costa or his people know where to find you, I'll be on the first flight out." John's promise brought her back to the present. "Okay?"

"Okay." Allison's tense muscles began to relax, and her breathing finally returned to normal. "Thank you."

"Just remember. It's business as usual unless you hear differently from me."

"I'll do my best."

"I know you will." His kind smile was almost audible. "Take care of yourself, Allyssa. I'll be in touch." And with that, John ended the call.

Allison—she refused to think of herself as Allyssa in her own home—slid the phone into her pocket to avoid missing John's expected text. Glancing around her modest apartment, she released a nervous breath as she made her way back over to her wall mounted T.V.

The news alert had ended, the daytime gameshow she'd been watching back in full swing.

Business as usual. Right.

Walking over to the sliding door leading to her small balcony, she carefully surveyed the street below. Allison watched as a red sports car drove by, followed by a white sedan.

A handful of people strolled this way and that down the well-maintained sidewalks of Main Street. The scene nearly the same as the day before, and the day before that.

Look at them down there. Walking around without a care in the world, completely oblivious to the fact that they were being watched.

Allison pulled the curtains closed. Next, she moved to those framing the small window to her right, followed by the ones hanging in her bedroom. After that, she went to her computer to look up information she prayed she'd never have to use.

Damn Lorenzo Costa for making her feel this way again. And damn Wade Crenshaw for talking her into testifying in the first place.

This isn't Wade's fault, and you know it.

Getting up from her computer desk chair, she plopped down on the edge of her bed. Fighting tears, she fell back onto her mattress and closed her eyes.

Truth be told, if she hadn't listened to Wade that night, she would've been killed a long time ago. But lately, it wasn't the night of the murder that haunted her dreams.

It was a different day. One that took place months later, after being forced to spend weeks hiding out under the watchful eye of the very Special Agent Crenshaw.

The same day Lorenzo Costa and Eddie Veneto were found guilty of murder.

And for a tiny, almost indiscernible moment, Allison

was foolish enough to think everything was going to be okay.

"I can't believe it's finally over."

"Believe it." Wade followed her into the D.A.'s private meeting room. *"You heard the judge. Thanks to you, those two are going away for life. They'll never be able to hurt you or anyone else ever again."*

Shutting the door behind him, he sauntered toward her. The corners of his tempting lips curved into that half-grin of his that always left her toes curling and her body aching with need.

"I was so nervous on that stand." She couldn't take her eyes off him. Though she tried, it was impossible not to notice how damn sexy he looked in his dark suit and tie.

Pride and something else she was afraid to name filled his gray gaze. Allison's stomach tingled, her heart thumping against her ribs as he ran his knuckles along the curve of her cheek.

"You did great, Allie." His deep voice rumbled. *"I'm so proud of you."*

"So what happens now?"

"That's up to you."

"It is?"

Wade nodded. "You're free now, sweetheart." He tucked a few wayward strands behind her ear. *"So you tell me...what is it you want?"*

Allison didn't even have to think about it. She knew exactly what she wanted, and for once in her life, she was going to take it.

"I can have anything I want?"

He dipped his handsome head in a slight nod. "Just name it, and it's yours."

Rising onto her tiptoes, she watched him closely for any signs that said she'd misread the chemistry between them. Allison smiled when the only thing she found reflected in his steely gaze was a primal heat matching her own.

. . .

"Allie..."

"You said it yourself, the case is over. You said I could have whatever I want." She brushed her lips against his. "I want you, Wade."

Strong hands slid down to her hips. Gripping her tightly, Wade pulled her wanton body flush with his.

Allison gasped, her breasts pushing against his muscled chest. The barrier her thin blouse created added to the tantalizing friction against her rock-hard nipples.

Fire flared behind his mesmerizing eyes, the slight scruff covering his jaw sending waves of goosebumps across her skin. "Sweetheart, I—"

The door opened, and Special Agent Ryan Landry rushed inside. "Wade, I need to—"

Wade dropped his hands and stepped to the side. The move was crushing, but Allison refused to let her disappointment show.

He clearly didn't want his partner to notice their intimate embrace, but it was too late. She could see it in the other man's blue eyes as they slid from Wade, to her, and back again.

"We need to talk." Ryan's expression was unnerving.

Allison took a step toward him. "What's wrong?" Because something was definitely wrong.=

"I, uh..." Ryan cleared his throat. "I just need a minute with Agent Crenshaw."

"Please. Is it Costa?" She refused to let him dismiss her so easily. "Did something happen with the verdict?"

"Allison, I really think it's best if I speak to Wade alone."

She was shaking her head before he was finished. "Tell me."

"Allie..." Wade's deep voice rumbled beside her. He put a comforting hand to the small of her back, but it did nothing to ease the sudden onslaught of nerves.

"No." She stepped out of his reach. "If this has to do with Costa's guilty verdict, I have a right to know!"

"It's not about the verdict." Sympathy softened Agent Landry's chiseled features as he ran a hand through his sandy blond hair. *"It's... Shit, Allie."* Ryan blew out a breath. *"It's your parents."*

Allison sucked in a breath. "My parents? W-what about them? Are they okay?"

But she knew before he ever said another word. It was there, in the way he was staring back at her. The way Wade quickly returned to her side.

"Their car was found in Hunting Creek, near the George Washington Memorial Parkway. Two women were jogging along the Mount Vernon Trail when they spotted it in the water."

"The water? Oh, my God. Well, did they get them out? Are they—"

"Allie, there were matching bullet wounds in the backs of your parents' heads." Ryan shook his head. *"Whoever did it executed them before pushing their car into the river. I'm sorry."*

"No!" Her head jerked from side to side with denial. *"No, no, no, no no!"*

She would've hit the ground had Wade not been there to catch her.

Time stood still as she broke down into a mess of tears and heartache. Wade held her tight, offering soothing words of sympathy and support she wasn't ready to hear.

After what felt like hours of uncontrollable sobbing, Allison drew in a stuttering breath, wiped her face dry, and pushed herself back to her feet. Feeling almost numb, she gathered her thoughts as best she could.

"He did this." Her voice was rough and ragged from crying. *"Lorenzo Costa killed my parents."*

The look of sympathy on Ryan's face made her physically sick to her stomach.

"The M.E.'s preliminary report shows an estimated time of death of approximately two hours ago." He spoke calmly. "Costa was in police custody on his way here for the reading of the verdict and sentencing. It couldn't have been him."

"Just because he didn't pull the trigger, that doesn't mean he isn't responsible. For Christ's sake, the man was just given a life sentence because he ordered the murder of my boss. And now..." Her voice cracked with heart shattering emotion. "And now, he's ordered the murder of my parents."

"For what end?"

"Revenge." Allison swiped angrily at a fallen tear. "This was his way of getting back at me for testifying against him."

"Or, it was a warning." Wade shared a look with his partner.

"You think I'm next?" She turned to him. "You think Costa plans to send someone after me, too?"

"I think Costa is a man who has a reputation to uphold." Worry swirled within the grays of his eyes. "Especially in prison. Word gets out that he allowed you to turn State's evidence against him without any sort of repercussion, he'll lose clout with the other prisoners."

"Not to mention the men he still has working for him on the outside," Ryan pointed out. To her, he said matter-of-factly, "They couldn't get to you before the trial, because you've been in protective custody. Now that the trial's over, Costa is going to make an example out of you. Starting with your parents, and ending with—"

"Me." Allison turned back to Wade. "He's going to kill me, too."

"I'm not going to let that happen." Wade held her shoulders in a gentle-yet-firm grip. "You hear me? No one is going to lay a hand on you."

"Protective detail is over, remember? I'm on my own now."

"Not necessarily." Ryan chimed back in. "There's one surefire *way to keep you safe from Costa's men. But it would mean becoming someone else entirely."*

Someone else? "You're talking about the Witness Protection Program, aren't you?"

He nodded. "And given the weight of your testimony, you'd be accepted into the Program, no questions asked."

"She'd have to leave her home." Wade pointed out the obvious. "Her family."

"I don't have a family. Not anymore." The truth in that statement nearly tore her in two.

"This wouldn't be like the protective custody you've been in up until now. WITSEC is different. You'd have to leave town. Go by a different name. Find a job unrelated to teaching, since that's the first place they'd start looking. You wouldn't be able to contact anyone from your past, or—"

"It's the best thing for her, Crenshaw." Ryan tried to convince his partner. "You know I'm right."

Allison watched Wade closely as he considered his partner's statement. She knew the second he came to the same conclusion as his partner.

He looked back to her. "You could enter the program in a temporary compacity. Just until we can finish bringing in the rest of Costa's crew."

"I have a funeral to plan." Her eyes welled, but she willed her tears not to fall. "Two funerals, actually. I can't just up and leave."

"Ryan's right, Allie. Costa will send people after you." His dark brows turned inward. "I'd lose my mind if anything ever happened to you. You should go."

"But I—"

"Now, Allie. You need to leave. Now."

The grip on her shoulders tightened. She frowned when he gave her a little shake.

"They're here, Allison. They're coming for you. You need to get

out." He shook her harder. "Now!"

ALLISON'S WOKE WITH A GASP. HER EYES FLEW OPEN, AND HER heart felt as though it was about to burst right out of her chest.

But as she took in the darkened room surrounding her, it became clear to her that she'd fallen asleep.

"Just a dream." She closed her eyes with an exhale. "It was just a stupid dream."

Actually, it was a memory. One that had been revisiting her more frequently lately.

Only *something* was off this time. Yes, she and Wade had nearly kissed that day. And yes, his partner had burst through the door with the horrifying news of her parents' death. But that last part, the part where Wade had been shaking her and yelling at her to leave…

That never happened.

Frowning, Allison was lying there, trying to make sense of the odd shift in the recurring dream when she heard a car door slam shut somewhere close outside. And then another.

Still feeling a bit out of sorts, she slid off the mattress and walked to the window. A tiny sliver of faded light shone through the slit separating the tweed panels, but it wasn't as bright as before. Dusk had arrived while she'd been sleeping, and the sun had nearly set.

Parting the curtains just enough to see outside, she glanced down to the street below. The third-floor apartment the U.S. Marshals had acquired for her sat over the small coffee shop-slash-bookstore where she'd worked since her move to Salado.

The small town's collection of local artists, nearby wineries, and eclectic shops drew in tourists from all over.

But the two men she saw walking across the street didn't seem like the usual kind of folks who chose this spot to visit.

It was probably a simple case of misplaced paranoia, but who could blame her? Between the news of Costa's escape and that strange turn of events in her dream, she felt completely out of sorts.

Rolling her eyes at herself, Allison started to pull the curtains close again, but stopped when a strong evening breeze blew one of the men's jackets open. She sucked in a breath when the man's shoulder holster and gun were revealed.

Wade's warning from her dream rolled through her head.

They're here, Allison. They're coming for you. You need to get out. Now!

Her heart flew into her throat. She closed the curtain and stumbled backward, away from the window.

Maybe those weren't Costa's men. Maybe they were sent to her by John.

John.

Allison swung her head around to look at the digital alarm clock by her bed. She was shocked to see that over four hours had passed since she'd spoken to him.

"He said he'd call," she spoke to herself as she pulled her phone from her pocket, praying she'd simply slept through her phone ringing.

Her shoulders fell when she saw there were no missed calls. He hadn't texted her, either. She decided to call him again.

With her phone to her ear, she went back over to the window. Taking a careful peek outside, she did her best not to be seen.

The men had just stepped onto the sidewalk. *Her* sidewalk. And when they disappeared from view, she knew they'd either entered the shop below, or they'd gone through the doorway next to it.

The one that accessed the staircase leading to her apartment.

Come on, John. Please pick up the phone.

But he didn't. Not the first time she tried. Or the second. Nor did he respond to the frantic text message her trembling fingers somehow managed to type.

Allison's breaths became shallow. Her lungs worked overtime to the point she was damn close to hyperventilating. But then a familiar sound reached her ears, forcing her to slow her breathing and listen.

The building was old and creaky, so even from all the way back here, she could always tell when someone had come through the upstairs door. There were only two apartments up here...hers and Shawna's,

Shawna Twill was the coffee shop's owner. She lived in a nicer, larger apartment across the narrow hall. But at this time of day, she'd be busy prepping to close.

For as long as Allison had worked for the sweet southern woman, she'd never seen Shawna leave the shop to come up to her apartment at this hour. Not once.

And if John had sent those men to protect her, he would've given her a heads up. Given the timing of it all—with Costa's escape having happened earlier that morning—the most probable explanation wasn't that they were here to keep her safe.

They were coming to kill her.

Allison's breathing picked up again. Her pulse spiked, and damn if fear hadn't left her frozen where she stood.

Snap out of it, Allie. You knew this could happen. You planned for it. Follow the plan.

Like a splash of cold water, her inner voice forced a calm she didn't truly feel. But it was right.

She'd lost everything because of this man and his goons. The job and life she loved. Her parents. She'd spent the last five years looking over her shoulder, just waiting for the next bad thing to happen. Because she knew it was only a matter of time.

Follow the plan.

Muffled male voices came from the other side of her door. Swallowing the giant knot of terror filling the base of her throat, Allison's socked feet were nearly silent as she carefully and swiftly went to her closet and pulled out the duffle hidden in the back corner.

One she'd had the aforethought to put together her first week here.

In it were extra clothes, a pair of running shoes, a small toiletry bag, and enough cash to get her by for a few days. She'd also thrown in a small first aid kit and can of pepper spray for added protection.

But even pepper spray would be no match for a gun.

Sliding the duffle strap over her shoulder, Allison tiptoed back to where she'd left her purse. Avoiding the spots in her floor she knew would creak, she tiptoed over to the kitchen bar, grabbed the purse, and practically ran over to the sliding glass doors leading to her balcony.

A knock on the door startled her, but by God's grace, she managed to stifle the squeal of surprise threatening to give her away.

"Miss Andrews, this is the U.S. Marshals. We need to speak with you."

The use of her real last name was just one of many red flags. One, anytime John spoke to her, he always, *always* used her alternative name. These guys were trained for that sort of thing.

Second, if those guys really were with the Marshal service, they wouldn't have announced themselves like that. It would be a dead giveaway that she was in the program and expose her to anyone within earshot.

And since they had no way of knowing for sure whether there was someone in the apartment across the hall...

No way in hell these guys are Marshals.

Praying she could open the door without making a sound, Allison kept the long curtains closed as she slid the lock loose. Sliding the door open as quickly and quietly as she could, she moved the curtain over just enough to allow her room to slide past and stepped outside.

After repositioning the curtain, she heard another knock. This one was harder. More forceful. So was the tone the man used with his second attempt at convincing her to open the door.

"We know you're in there, Miss Andrews," the man hollered through the wooden barrier. "There's been a development in your case we need to discuss. It's urgent, so please open the door."

Not a chance.

Carefully closing the door behind her, she slid the small crossbody purse up over her head before snaking her arm through the strap. With it and her duffle bag resting against her hip, she turned and reached for the release latch to the gate separating the balcony from the fire escape attached to the north side.

The building's first floor housed the shop, the second was used for storage, which left the top floor for the two apartments.

Pushing the wrought-iron gate open, Allison cringed when the gate's metal hinges squeaked as they turned. Knowing it was unavoidable, she drew in a breath, shoved it the rest of the way open, and started down the white spiral staircase.

She was halfway between the third and second floors when she heard the muted sound of her door being kicked in.

With her fear icing her veins, Allison ignored the bite from the metal against the soles of her socked feet and ran down the spiraled steps as fast as she could. Her sliding door opened at the same time she reached the bottom.

"There she is!"

Looking up, she saw one of the two men staring down at her. Tall and thin with jet black hair, the man stared down at her with the same cold, emotionless expression Lorenzo Costa had worn the night he killed Rick.

But what turned her blood cold was the gun in his hand. Complete with a long, black suppressor.

Oh, God!

With her two bags bouncing awkwardly against her hip and leg, Allison took off across the street in a dead sprint. Her car was parked along the sidewalk across from her apartment, two spaces behind the fake U.S. Marshals' car.

She pressed the key fob to unlock her doors. At the same time, a bullet whizzed past her head. She screamed and ducked, nearly dropping her keys in the process.

But didn't dare stop.

Reaching her car, Allison grabbed the handle and started to pull the door open. Glass shattered as another bullet struck the driver's side window. Fire lanced across her upper left arm, but she pushed past the flash of pain, tossed her bags into the passenger seat, and dove into the car.

With trembling fingers, she inserted the key into the ignition. Another bullet slammed into her door, just below the window's edge, the sound of metal pinging off metal making her jump.

The engine revved to life. Shoving the gearshift into reverse, she backed up just enough to squeeze past the car in front of her. Then she took off like a bat out of Hell.

Tires squealed, and the few people still out and about turned and stared, but she kept her eyes on the road and sped away. Two blocks later, she turned left, her car bouncing over potholes in the alley between the town's bank and a realtor's office.

Allison glanced in her rearview, relieved when she didn't see anyone following her. They would be, though. Of that, she had no doubt.

Stick to the plan, Al. You've got this.

One of the first things Allison did when she first moved here was to map out several escape routes. Each originating from different places around town. Just in case.

Because deep down, she'd always known this day would come.

The path she was on now took her down the alley before backtracking to her left. Speeding down the road behind her building, Allison prayed the men after her would think she'd continued north.

The success of her plan depended on it.

Periodically checking her rearview, she continued down the two-lane road. Turning right at the stop sign, she was more than a little grateful to find the road leading south of town empty.

Thank God for Mondays.

The first day of the week in Salado was always the slowest. It didn't hurt that most of the town's citizens were already home for the night.

Sparing a quick glance down, Allison sucked in a breath

when she saw blood dripping down her arm from where the asshole's bullet had grazed her. Now that she'd seen the gash with her own eyes, the white-hot pain intensified.

Still, she kept on.

Street by street, turn by terrifying turn, Allison weaved her way through the quieter parts of town. Blood loss and fear left her shaken and nauseated, but she refused to stop until she got to where she was going.

Finally, after what felt like hours later, her intended spot came into view.

She checked her mirror again, relieved to find nothing but a cloud of dust behind her as she turned onto a gravel road. With no one else around, Allison pushed the accelerator to the floor and drove toward one of four locations she'd previously designated as a safe spot.

Half a mile later, her heart shot into her throat as the back of the car fishtailed when she turned onto another, less-traveled road. Adrenaline and fear threatened to take over, but Allison stayed the course until she came to her destination.

A railway bridge that hovered high over a large stretch of grassland.

She'd heard rumors of couples using the secluded spot to park and make out. Thankfully, even the teenagers in town had decided to call it an early night.

Pulling the car behind one of the bridge's two massively large, concrete pillars, Allison put it in park and turned off the ignition. Using the structure to hide her within the shadows of the night.

Sweat beaded on her forehead, the pain in her arm becoming more noticeable. She needed to call John again, but first things first.

Stop the bleeding.

Allison reached for her go-bag, unzipped it with one

hand. Grabbing the plastic first aid kit, she set it in her lap and unlatched the two clips. Inside were several different sizes of bandages, antiseptic wipes, antibiotic ointment, a pair of tweezers, and a few other items.

After a quick glance at the wound. Later, once she was someplace safe, she'd clean herself up and redress the wound. But for now, one of the four-inch by four-inch bandages would have to do.

Using her teeth, she ripped open the package and pulled out the sterile bandage. As best she could, Allison then placed the padded part over the long gash, hissing through the pain when she pressed against it to secure its hold.

Once the bandage was in place, she put the empty wrapper into the case and closed it shut before tossing it back over with her bag.

Giving herself a minute to regroup, Allison let her head fall back against the headrest. With her eyes closed, she did her best to breathe past the pain. The fear.

How the hell did they find me so fast?

Lorenzo Costa's reach was endless. One of the many facts she'd learned about the horrible man during his trial. Still, he'd only just escaped this morning. Yet, here she was, running for her life less than twelve hours later?

Something wasn't adding up.

Call John.

Trembling from the adrenaline still racing through her system, Allison got out her phone and tapped John's number. Like before, it rang and rang, eventually going to voicemail.

"John, it's me. They found me! I-I don't know who they are, but two men just showed up at my apartment and shot at me! I'm at a safe place for now, but I need help. I need to get out of here! Please call me!"

By the end of the call, tears were streaming down her cheeks. She looked at the name of the other contact—considered calling it, even. It was a number she'd entered into her phone after John told her the man in charge of the case in D.C. had transferred to Denver.

On a whim, she'd looked up the number to the FBI office and entered it into her contacts. Just in case. Now here she was, thinking about actually *calling* that same number while hiding out from men who wanted to kill her.

In the end, she decided to give John a few minutes to respond before going down that particular rabbit hole. Ten minutes later, she sucked up her pride and made the call.

"Denver Federal Bureau of Investigation, how may I direct your call?"

Allison opened her mouth, then shut it again. Her chest moved up and down with heaving breaths as she contemplated whether or not this was the right move. Apparently, she waited too long.

"Hello?" The female voice spoke up again. "Is anyone there?"

Crap. "I'm here! Sorry. I-I need to speak with Special Agent Wade Crenshaw." Belatedly, she added, "I have information about the Lorenzo Costa case."

Praying he was even in the office at this hour—and that last bit would coax the operator to put her right through—Allison held her breath and waited.

"One moment, please."

A minute later, a man she thought she'd never talk to again answered on the first ring.

"Crenshaw."

Allison sucked in a breath. Just like five years ago, his voice created a sense of calm she'd never been able to replicate. A fact that would've driven her crazy had she had time to really think about it. Given her current situation, there were much bigger issues at hand.

"W-Wade?"

A slight pause and then, "Allie?"

Surprised he recognized her voice, she swallowed against the slew of emotions just hearing his voice created. "Yeah. It's me."

"Are you okay? You sound upset."

Understatement of the year.

"No." She shook her head and swiped at a fresh round of tears. "No, I'm not okay. They found me, Wade. I-I don't know how, but they showed up at my apartment with guns. I tried calling John, but h-he won't pick up. I-I'm scared and alone…and I didn't know who else to call."

"Who found you?" She heard what sounded like the snapping of fingers. "Sweetheart, I need you to take a breath and slow down. Now, tell me exactly what happened."

Gritting her teeth at the frustrating term of endearment, Allison ignored the fiery pain in her arm and gave him the shortened version.

"Where are you?" His tone was low. Deadly.

"I-I'm hiding out by a bridge just outside of Salado, Texas. That's the town they moved me to after…" She let her voice trail off, knowing he'd understand.

"Texas?" Another man's voice reached her ears. Someone with Wade said something before he asked her, "Ask her how far Salado is from Dallas."

"How far are you from Dallas?" Wade asked the other man's question.

"I-I don't know. A couple hours, maybe?"

Another pause. "Did the men who came to your apartment see which direction you went?"

"I don't know." Her face threatened to crumble, but she

bit her lip to stave off more tears. "I-I don't think so. I took a lot of different turns before coming here."

"Good girl. Now, I need you to listen carefully, okay? My partner has a contact in Dallas. He's a detective my partner knows and trusts. He's on the phone with him now." A few seconds went by while he spoke to a man she assumed was the partner. Then he was back. "Allie, listen to me. Detective Eric West, the man my partner knows, is already on his way to you right now. It's going to take him a couple hours to get there, so I need you to stay put and wait for him. Once Detective West gets there, he's going to take you someplace safe until I can get to you."

Her heart gave a hard thump, relief nearly flooding her. "You're coming here, too?"

"Yes." Lowering his voice, he told her, "You just keep yourself safe until I can get there, okay?"

"Okay." She was about to end the call but stopped at the last second. "Wait! H-how will I know the man is who he says he is?"

The phone went quiet as Wade presumably considered her question. When he spoke again, his voice was lower. Softer.

"Do you remember that night at the safe house? The night we stayed up watching movies and talking?"

How could she forget. It was the same night she realized she'd fallen in love with the handsome protector.

"I remember," Allison whispered.

"You asked me what my favorite movie was. Do you remember the answer I gave?"

"Spaceballs." Allison couldn't help but smile.

She'd expected him to say some macho action film or crime drama. When he mentioned the 1980's Star Wars spoof, she'd burst out laughing.

But only because she loved that movie, too.

"That's right. Now, when Detective West gets there, I want you to ask him what my favorite movie is. That way, you'll know it's safe to go with him."

Okay, that was actually a good idea.

"Allie? You still with me?"

"Yeah." She answered a bit too loudly. "I'm here."

"Stay alert and out of sight. If you need anything, call me at this number."

"Okay."

"And sweetheart?"

God, she hated the way he sounded when he called her that. All smooth and loving. As if he actually cared.

"Yeah?"

In that same deep, rumbly voice of his, Wade ended the conversation by promising, "I'll see you soon."

3

Wade had flown to many places in his life. Mexico. Europe. From the east coast to the west. But somehow, the two-and-a-half-hour flight from Denver to Dallas was the longest he'd ever experienced.

It didn't help that it had taken over two hours to get everything arranged. Things like coming up with a safe and reliable plan to get Allie to safety. Purchasing a plane ticket. Getting the green light from his boss to take the time off.

Not that he or anyone else could've stopped him from getting to her.

Surprisingly, SAC Hunt not only understood the situation, but the guy even flipped the bill for the trip. Technically, the Federal Bureau of Investigations was covering his travel expenses, but still. Having his boss's full support made things a hell of a lot easier.

Probably still feels bad about my having almost bit the big one five months ago.

Wade resisted the urge to rub the spot where a serial killer's bullet damn near killed him five months earlier.

Lucky for him, his partner had showed up before he could bleed out.

His wound had fully healed, but the scar was a constant reminder of how close he came to dying. And how short life really was. It was also one of the reasons he was so determined to make things right with Allie.

Starting tonight.

He'd screwed things up five years ago by putting his high-profile case above all else. Including her. But that was all in the past.

Until tonight, Wade had used her admission into WITSEC as his chance to make a clean break. Not because he didn't care about her, like she most likely believed. Because he *did*.

Hard as it was, Wade had fully committed to his personal vow to leave her alone and let her have the life she deserved. He never pushed for more. Never used his personal or professional resources to try to figure out where she'd been placed. Never once attempted to contact her. All in an effort to keep her safe.

And up until now, it had worked.

He could still hear the trembling in her voice when she'd called him. Could practically *feel* the terror Allie must have felt as she ran away from certain death.

She was supposed to be safe. She should've been fucking safe!

"Goddamnit!" Wade smacked the palm of his hand against the rental car's steering wheel.

This was his fault. He'd been young and naïve, and had done his best to put her out of his mind because he believed the system would keep her safe

He'd never forgive himself for having gravely underestimated Lorenzo Costa's need for revenge. Allie's parents had been brutally *murdered* on their way to the courthouse for the sole purpose of extracting revenge on her for testifying.

So on that fateful day five years ago, he'd convinced himself that letting her go without a fight was the absolute right decision. Now, he knew differently.

He understood that Costa had simply been biding his time. Waiting for the perfect opportunity to make his move. To go after the one person responsible for ruining his life.

Hence today's attack.

Wade gripped the leather steering wheel to the point he thought it might break. Drawing in a deep breath, he had to force himself to remember that she was okay. That Detective West was with her, and that she was *okay*.

Please let her be okay.

Loosening his death grip, he weaved his rental car in and out of traffic. Though he'd already called the man guarding Allie the minute he'd landed, Wade decided to call again to let the other man—and Allie—know he was close.

"West," Detective West answered right away.

"It's me. GPS shows me fifteen minutes from the hotel." *Still too fucking long.*

"Sounds good," West sounded calm enough. "We just got settled. Room four twenty-three."

Putting more pressure on the gas pedal, Wade released a slow, controlled breath of relief. "How is she?"

"Shaken up, but that's to be expected."

No shit. "She need anything? Clothes, or food?"

"She had a go-bag ready, and I just ordered her some room service."

The fact that Allie had a go-bag ready didn't surprise him in the least. "Let her know I'm almost there."

"Will do."

Thirteen minutes later, he was walking through the

hotel's entrance with his own bag hung over his shoulder. After a slow-as-fuck elevator ride, he finally reached Allie's room.

Tapping his knuckles against the door, Wade waited for West to answer. A shadow filled the peephole seconds before the door cracked open.

"It's me." He held up his official FBI I.D.

After a thorough once-over, the brown-haired man opened the door fully. Showing him the same courtesy, Detective West held up his badge and I.D. before stepping aside. "Come on in."

"Thanks." Wade slid past the other man. Stepping fully into the room, his eyes frantically scanned the modest, double queen bedroom. He didn't see her.

"She's in the shower," West seemed to read his mind. "Needed a few minutes to decompress after what happened."

Yeah, he supposed she did.

Turning back around, he rubbed a hand over his jaw and faced the other man. "Was she able to give a description of the men who came to her apartment?"

"Only saw one. Tall, thin, dark hair and eyes." The other man sighed. "You know, when Noah called, he failed to mention those bastards shot her."

The fuck?

"She was *hit*?" Wade's eyes grew wide, his jaw going slack as he stumbled back a step.

When he'd spoken with her on the phone, she'd sounded scared, but never mentioned being hurt. And when he'd called West to let him know he'd landed at DFW, the asshole hadn't said a fucking word about Allie being injured.

"Relax, Crenshaw. It's just a graze."

Wade didn't give a rat's ass if it was a fucking splinter. The idea of her being hurt in any way gutted him. Knowing she'd been *shot?*

He dropped his bag onto the floor. Spinning on his heels, his first instinct was to go to her. He made it two wide steps across the room's plush carpet before West's voice of reason broke through his whirling thoughts.

"Not sure that's a good idea."

Wade's steps halted. He swung back around. "What?"

The Dallas detective shrugged casually. "I mean, you can barge in there if you want, but I'm pretty sure the lady would like to finish her shower in peace. Unless you two are—"

"We're not," he rushed to answer.

Shit. He'd been so focused on seeing for himself that Allie really was okay, he'd momentarily forgot she was in the shower. Which meant she was naked.

Of its own accord, a flash from one of Wade's many fantasies broke through his panic. One of Allie in the shower. Water dripping down her luscious nude body while he...

"Right." West shoved his hands into his pockets. "Of course."

Something about the way the man spoke sent Wade immediately on the defensive. Spine straightened, he marched back over to where the detective stood. Invading his personal space, he made sure the asshole knew the truth.

"I was the lead agent on the case against the man Allie helped to put away," he spat out. "I protected her until the trial was over, and I haven't seen her since. And before you ask, *Detective*, when it came to that woman in there, I conducted myself with the utmost professionalism."

Minus the almost-kiss right before she was whisked away, but that was beside the point.

"Whoa. Easy, man." West lifted his hands, palms up. "I didn't mean to imply otherwise."

Breathing through his nose, Wade slowly regained control of his hair-trigger anger. "Sorry," he offered his new acquaintance. "Guess I'm just…"

"Worried," West finished for him. "It's okay, man. I get it."

From the look in the other man's eyes, Wade believed he just might.

With a curt nod, he got out of the man's face and took a step back. It registered that the water was no longer running seconds before he heard the door behind him open.

Turning his head, he found himself staring into a set of beautiful blue eyes he hadn't seen for half a decade. They were bloodshot, as if she'd recently been crying, and there were dark shadows marring the delicate skin below.

But even with all that, they still took his breath away.

"Hi." Her voice sounded small. Weary.

"Hey." Wade took a hesitant step forward.

They stood there, staring at each other as if the world around them had vanished. Probably would've *kept* staring if West hadn't just cleared his throat behind him.

"Okay, so…I'm gonna head on home." The detective pointed his thumb toward the door behind him. "You know, since you're here." He looked at Wade. "And you're obviously in capable hands." His gaze shifted to Allie. "You need anything, though…*either* of you…all you have to do is call."

"Thank you, Detective West," Allie offered softly.

"It's Eric." The man smiled. "And no need to thank me. I'm just glad you made it out of there in one piece."

"I'll see you out." Wade started for the door. Offering his hand, he said, "I can't thank you enough."

"Like I said, just glad she's okay." West shook his hand. "Besides, your partner was a big help when he worked that case with us a few months back. Least I could do was return the favor." Sliding a quick glance in Allie's direction, he lowered his voice for Wade's ears only. "She didn't say much on the drive here, but I'm familiar with the case. That girl's been through hell. Take good care of her, yeah?"

"I plan to." Wade dropped his hand back to his side. He didn't need this man, or anyone else, telling him what he needed to do. Not when it came to the woman behind him.

As far as he was concerned, she was his, now. He may have fucked things up with her before by putting the case above all else. But this time...*this* time, she was only thing that mattered.

West stepped into the hall. Wade was about to shut the door when the man turned back around at the last second.

"Oh, and one more thing I forgot to ask."

"What's that?"

The guy's blue eyes shimmered with humor, his brows furrowing slightly. "Spaceballs? Really?"

Wade smirked. "What can I say? Mel Brooks is a comedic genius."

Shoulders shaking with a healthy chuckle, West gave him a parting wave and disappeared down the hall. The door snicked shut behind him, and suddenly Wade found himself standing in a hotel room with the woman who'd haunted his dreams.

"I wasn't sure you'd come."

The soft whisper of a comment had him spinning on his heels. Allie was still standing in the exact same spot, her arms crossed at her center as if she were holding herself.

It should be me. I should be the one holding her.

For the first time since she'd stepped out of the bathroom, he really looked at her. She'd lost some weight since he'd last seen her. Of course, living a life constantly looking over your shoulder could do that to a person.

Allie was dressed in a pair of black yoga pants with a matching tank top that gave him the slightest peek of skin between her waistband and the shirt's hem.

His fingers twitched with the urge to go to her. To touch her there and feel the skin he knew would be feather soft. Until he noticed the large white bandage on her left upper arm.

Releasing a low curse, Wade covered the distance between them. With his six-two frame towering over her, he used a gentle hold around her left wrist to lift her arm and study the bandaged area.

"It's just a scratch," she told him. "The bullet grazed me as I was getting into my car."

His back teeth ground together. A graze was more than a simple scratch. They also hurt like hell.

The bastard who did this to you will pay for this, sweetheart. If it's the last thing I do.

"You take anything for the pain?" Wade did his best to keep the anger toward the men who'd tried to kill her at bay.

"Eric got me some Tylenol from the gift shop downstairs."

"Good." He nodded, his thumb absentmindedly brushing her smooth skin.

"What happens now?"

Though he wanted nothing more than to keep touching her, Wade released his hold on her arm and lifted his gaze to hers. "For tonight, we'll stay here so you can get some rest. First thing tomorrow, we'll head to Denver."

"You're taking me to Colorado?" Allie's blue eyes grew wide. "Why?"

"Because that's where I'll be. And until Costa and his crew are stopped, I'm not letting you out of my sight."

"Why?"

He frowned. "What do you mean, why?"

With a shrug of her shoulders, she stepped past him and walked toward one of the room's two beds. "Why'd you drop everything to come here? You could've just as easily sent another agent." Allie turned back around to face him. "I mean, you've never once bothered to call or check in on me since I left that day, and if you're not in D.C. anymore, then this isn't even your case anymore, right? So I guess what I'm asking is, why does it matter what happens to me?"

Jesus, she really had no idea how important she was to him, did she?

How could she? Not like you ever told her.

No, he hadn't. And now wasn't exactly the time, but the least he could do was give her something.

Walking over to where she stood, he stopped directly in front of her. And with an intent stare he prayed helped her see the truth, he said, "I didn't come here because of the case. I came because I couldn't bare the thought of something happening to you."

Shaking her head, she started to say, "You don't have to—"

"What I'm doing...coming here, taking you back with me to Denver? I'm doing it because it matters." He reached up, gently cupping her face with one hand. "Because *you* matter."

"Wade..." She sounded breathless, her pupils dilating as he spoke.

She was still as affected by his touch as she was the last time he saw her. Good to know.

"Get some rest, sweetheart." He dropped his hand and took a step back. "We've got a long day ahead of us tomorrow."

Before he did something stupid, like pull her in his arms and kiss her, Wade turned around and headed for his bag. He picked it up and headed for the bathroom to shower, but before he closed the door, he turned back and said, "Anyone knocks on the door, you come get me."

Still looking somewhat shocked by their intimate exchange, she nodded but said nothing. Wade started to shut the door behind him but decided to leave it cracked in case she needed him.

Truth was, he *wanted* her to need him. Not because the bad guys were after her, though he'd gladly die if it meant keeping her safe. But as he stood under the steaming water, he realized what, deep down, he already knew.

Wade wanted Allie to want him the same way he'd always wanted her. As a partner. A lover. And someday, if he could find a way to convince her, something much more.

By the time he stepped out of the bathroom, the lights were off, and she was sound asleep. Walking silently to where she lay, Wade couldn't help but brush some hair from her face and stare.

Damn, she was beautiful. Even more so than he remembered. And as he continued to stare, her words from before rolled through his head.

I wasn't sure you'd come.

That she'd even doubted him for a second broke his heart. There was a time when she'd trusted him completely. And there, standing by her sleeping form, Wade made a solemn vow to do whatever it took to earn that trust back.

Unable to resist, he leaned down and pressing his lips to her temple. "I'll always come for you, sweetheart," he whispered. Then he walked over to his bag, grabbed his gun, and headed for the bed closest to the door.

Placing the weapon on the nightstand, Wade set the alarm on his phone before crawling under the covers. With one final glance at the woman he wished was in his bed, he closed his eyes and went to sleep.

4

I'll always come for you, sweetheart.

With Wade's words playing on a torturous loop, Allison stared out the car window as the scenery passed her by. He'd whispered them to her when he thought she was asleep.

Of course, he thought that because that's what she'd *wanted* him to believe.

After everything that had happened—the shooting, being whisked away by a detective she'd never met before, seeing Wade again after all this time—it had simply been too much to deal with.

So she'd taken advantage of his time in the shower, and decided not to deal with *any* of it just then. Especially him.

God, it had been so hard, though. When they'd been standing by her bed and he'd cupped her cheek the way he had, there'd been a moment she could've sworn he was going to kiss her. And when he'd stared down at her with those soul-reaching eyes and said she mattered to him...

I wanted to kiss him.

She honestly just might have, too, if he hadn't backed away when he had. In that moment, she hadn't been able to decide whether she was happy he'd broken the spell, or disappointed.

The worst part of the whole thing was, she should be thinking about how to stay alive, not whether or not she should have kissed the man who'd put her in this position in the first place.

Stop blaming him, Al. None of this is his fault.

Once again, the tiny voice in her head was right. Bad timing had sent her out into the alley that night. And while Wade had done his best to persuade her to testify at Costa's trial, ultimately, the choice had been hers.

Her parents had paid the ultimate price for that choice. A heartwrenching consequence Allison would have to live with for the rest of her life.

"You hungry?" Wade's rumbly voice reached her from the driver's seat.

Keeping her eyes focused on the scenery outside, she muttered, "Not really."

"When was the last time you ate?"

Allison straightened her head, but still kept her gaze forward. She thought for a moment, trying to remember.

"I'm not sure. Yesterday morning, I think?" Her response came out like a question. Something Wade picked up on immediately.

"That settles it. There's a town up ahead. I saw a billboard for a diner there. We'll grab a bite to refuel, then head back out."

She didn't bother arguing, because it wouldn't do any good. A lesson she'd learned early on when he'd first taken over her protective detail prior to the trial.

Once Wade Crenshaw made up his mind, there wasn't much changing it.

Besides, he was probably right. They'd been on the road a few hours, and she needed to keep up her strength. If for no other reason than to be able to run again if the situation arose.

Allison sighed. God, she was so tired of this. The running and hiding. A secret life with a secret identity.

All she wanted, more than anything in the world, was to be free to live whatever life *she* chose. To live where she wanted and use her real name in public. To have the option to teach again...

To find love and raise a family.

The thought had her sneaking a sideways glance toward the man sitting to her left. Just as quickly, she blinked, refocusing on the road in front of her.

In her dreams, Wade was always the man Allison imagined herself settling down with. And when she pictured herself as a bride, it was his face she saw waiting at the end of the aisle.

But those were just fantasies. The sexy FBI agent had long ago forgotten about her. In fact, the only reason he was here now was because he felt a professional obligation. Except...

I didn't come here because of the case. I came because I couldn't bear the thought of something happening to you.

Wade had sounded so sincere when he'd said those words to her last night. And the emotions filling his gaze when he'd told her she mattered to him...

It was almost enough to make her believe him.

But Allison had been down this road once before. Well, almost. Then her parents were murdered, and she was put into the WITSEC program. A pretty effective end to what might have been.

"Here we are." Wade's deep voice broke through her wandering thoughts.

As he parked the car, she studied the quaint diner's exterior. It wasn't large, but given the many cars in the parking lot, the place was a popular lunch spot for the area.

Once inside, they were seated in a booth toward the back wall. Remembering Wade always liked facing the door, Allison automatically slid onto the cushioned seat on the other side.

He smiled but didn't comment. It was a good thing, too, since she had no idea how she would've responded had he brought it up.

"Here are your menus." The young lady who'd greeted them laid two laminated menus onto the table in front of them. "We serve breakfast and lunch all day, so everything on there is available to order. I'll go grab some water for y'all while you look them over."

"Thank you." Allison offered her a tiny smile. Shivering, she rubbed her hands together a bit before picking up the menu to make her selection.

"You cold?"

She glanced across the table. "A little, but I'm fine."

"I have a jacket in the car. I can go get it if you want."

"No, I'm good." She shook her head. "Thanks, though."

It was a kind offer, but the last thing she needed was to have his woodsy male scent surrounding her more than it already did. Her faded blue jeans and gray hoodie would have to do.

Before today, Allison had never given much thought as to what she'd packed in her go-bag. But this morning, in the privacy of the hotel room's bathroom, she'd had found herself wishing she'd packed something a little nicer. Or at least less frumpy.

Instead, she was dressed like a college student after a long night out. Messy bun, included. Wade, on the other hand, looked like sin on a stick.

With his well-worn jeans that fit snuggly across his taut ass and toned thighs and the dark gray V-neck tee that showcased his magnificent male form, she had to physically force herself not to stare.

"Here ya go." Their server returned. As promised, she'd brought them each a large glass of ice water. "Have you had enough time to pick, or do you need a few more minutes?"

"I'm good." Wade looked to her. "You know what you want, or do you need more time to look it over?"

"I'm fine." Not really, but she quickly chose the first thing that sounded halfway decent. "I'll have the grilled chicken sandwich and a salad."

"Okay." The young lady jotted down her order before turning her attention to Wade. "And for you?"

"I think I'm going to go with the tenderloin and fries."

"Alrighty. Either of you want something other than water to drink?"

"I'm good." Allie shook her head.

"Actually, I'd love a Diet Coke."

"Pepsi okay?"

"Even better."

The young woman wrote down his drink order. "I'll get that Pepsi, and your food will be ready shortly."

"Thank you," both Allison and Wade spoke in unison.

A second later, the sweet server was gone.

"So." Wade finally broke through the uncomfortable silence. "Minus the last twenty-four hours, how have you been?"

You'd know if you'd bothered to call.

"Fine." Allison lied. "You?"

"Oh, you know. Just spending my days chasing bad guys."

"Why Colorado?" she found herself asking.

The question seemed to surprise him. Settling against the booth's cushioned back, he said, "I, uh...I don't know. Guess after everything that happened, I felt like I needed a fresh start. I'd been offered the position shortly after Costa's arrest, but hadn't really considered taking it until—"

He cut himself short, which made her that much more curious.

"Until what?"

With an audible swallow, Wade looked her straight in the eye and said, "Until you left."

Her heart gave a hard thump against her ribs. He'd left because of her? That couldn't be right.

"I didn't leave because I wanted to."

"I know." He nodded his handsome head. "And I'm glad you went into the program, because it's kept you safe."

Allison released a very unladylike scoff. "Until now."

"We're going to catch these guys, Al." He leaned forward, resting his elbows on the table. "We did it once before, remember?"

"Yeah, I remember." She straightened her spine. "I also remember what happened after."

"Allie..."

"My parents were murdered, Wade. All because of a choice I made. And I couldn't even go to their funeral because the Bureau decided it was too much of a risk."

Though John had agreed to drive by the cemetery service on their way out of town. But that was only because she'd threatened to run the first chance she got if he didn't.

"I know." Sympathy filled his dark stare. "I'm sorry."

"Are you?"

The question had Wade's face drawing down into a serious frown. "Of course, I am. It killed me to know you were out there somewhere, dealing through all that pain and grief alone."

Allison didn't know what was happening, but the more he talked, the angrier she got.

"Well, maybe if you'd, I don't know...bothered to check in with me, I wouldn't have felt so alone."

Needing to be anywhere but stuck in that booth with him, she slid out of her seat and stormed toward the diner's entrance. Wade hollered after her, followed by a promise to their server that they'd be back, but she ignored him.

Him and the multitude of strange looks she was getting from the business's other customers. And she didn't stop until she was nearly half a block away.

Feeling as though she couldn't catch her breath, Allison bent over at the waist. With her hands on her knees, she stayed like that. Willing herself to calm down. It didn't work. Nothing did.

Not until...

A warm hand pressed against her back.

"Slow down, sweetheart." Wade's soothing voice enveloped her. "That's it. Breath in through your nose, out through your mouth."

Despite her desire to tell him to leave her alone, Allison did as she was told. Following his lead, she breathed in and out slowly, repeating the move until she no longer felt like her anxiety was off the rails.

"That a girl." He rubbed the palm of his hand along her back. "There you go."

Allison stood straight and stepped out of his reach. Not

because she didn't like what he was doing, but because she did.

Too much.

"Better?"

"Yeah." The bun on the top of her head wobbled with a jerky nod. "Thanks."

"I'm sorry."

"For what?"

"Not contacting you after you left."

"It's okay." She lied. "I mean, the case was over, right? Plus, I'm sure you were busy, what with the move and all."

Allison knew she sounded like a spoiled brat, but she couldn't seem to help herself. She'd once had an amazing connection with this man. One unlike any she'd ever felt before.

After losing the only family she had—especially in such a violent manner—Wade was the only person she wanted to be around. The only person she *needed*. And he hadn't been there.

No matter how justified or logical his reasons, she'd never gotten past that.

"That's not why I never called." Wade took a step toward her.

Crossing her arms in front of her, Allison forced herself to look him in the eye. "I get it. I wasn't supposed to have any contact from my life before, and you were a part of that life." Even if only for a little bit. "Plus, you probably didn't even know where I was, so..."

That's what she'd told herself every time she sat alone in her tiny apartment, willing the phone to ring.

"I have contacts in the Marshals service. I could've found out where you were."

Allison's brows bunched together. "You know, if this is

your way of trying to defend yourself, you're doing a pretty shitty job of it."

His eyes lit up with humor, and his broad shoulders shook with a low chuckle. "God, I've missed you."

"I don't need platitudes, Wade. I just needed…"

"What?"

You. "Nothing." She sidestepped him and started toward the diner. "Our food's probably sitting on the table getting cold, so we should head back inside before—"

A gentle hand to her wrist had her stopping in her tracks. Swinging back around, Allison was taken completely off guard when Wade pulled her body flush with his.

"What are you—"

Wade gave her no warning before he slammed his mouth to hers.

On reflex, Allison started to pull away, but Wade wasn't having it. He wrapped his strong arms around her and held her close.

Within seconds, she was melting against him. Taking every ounce of what the man had to offer.

Holy God, Special Agent Wade Crenshaw can kiss!

Needing more, Allison opened her mouth to invite him in. The second she did, his tongue met hers with a fiery, unbridled passion. She wasn't sure how long they stood like that, tasting and savoring each other for the very first time.

And she didn't care.

All too soon, Wade was ending the kiss as he seemed to come to his senses. Feeling almost dazed, Allison stared up at him as she licked her swollen lips. Still tasting him there.

His heated gaze bore deep into hers as he cupped her face with both hands and rasped, "I've never given you platitudes, sweetheart, and I'm not about to start now. The only thing that kept me from contacting you…from *coming* to you…was knowing that doing so could put you at even greater risk."

"Wade?"

Resting his forehead against hers, his hot breath hit her chin as he said, "I know I failed you, sweetheart. In more ways than one. But that's over now, you hear me? I've got you back, and I'm not ever letting you go again."

Holy smokes. Did he really just say what she thought he said? Allison had to be sure.

"What are you saying?"

"I'm saying, I've never felt about anyone the way I feel about you. I know this is crazy, and we may have been apart for the last five years, but I've never stopped thinking about you. Not once." He pressed his lips to hers in a soft, gentle kiss. "My timing sucks, and we need to deal with the whole Costa situation first, but after… After, I'd really like it if we could give this thing between us a chance." Looking adorably nervous, he added, "Please tell me I'm not alone in this."

The entire time they were apart, Allison had been torn between loving him…and hating him. But standing here, wrapped in his loving embrace, and hearing the words she'd forever longed to hear, there was only one thing she had to say.

"You're not alone, Wade." She rose onto her tiptoes and kissed *him*. "You're not alone."

After giving her another brief but wonderful taste, he pulled away and linked his fingers with hers. "I don't know about you, but I'm suddenly famished."

Laughing, Allison didn't bother to think about how foreign the sound felt coming from her chest, or how insane the last twenty-four-plus hours had been. Nor did she stop to analyze what had just transpired between her and the very special Agent Crenshaw.

For once in her screwed-up life, the only thing on Allison's mind was the decision to throw caution to the wind and take what she wanted. And what she wanted—more than anything—was the man holding her hand in his and walking beside her.

5

Denver's FBI field office, two days later...

Wade stared at the door to his unit's office space, willing Allie to walk through it.

"Would you stop worrying?" Noah walked over to him. "She and Maggie are just right downstairs getting some coffee."

Yeah, and your wife was damn near killed in the basement of this same building.

Not wanting to dredge up the horrible memory for his friend, Wade chose to go with a lie. "I'm not worried."

"Oh really?" His partner of four years smirked, his dark eyes gleaming with humor. "Funny, 'cause that's the fifth time I've caught you checking the door in the past ten minutes."

Shit. For a second there, he forgot Noah was one of the sharpest agents in the Bureau. The guy was also his best friend.

Sitting down at his desk, Wade picked up the file he'd

put together on Costa and his crew. Pretending to read it over, he acted as if the other man's words didn't bother him in the least.

Except they did.

With a frustrated sigh, he dropped the folder and looked back up at Noah. "Okay, fine. So I'm worried. But can you blame me? I'm harboring an active participant of WITSEC, not to mention the woman's got a target on her back the size of Texas."

"You call the Marshals to tell them where she is yet?"

"No."

"Why not?"

"Because, I don't want her to..." Wade stopped short of admitting the truth. "Look, I'm just trying to keep her safe, okay?"

"Uh, huh."

"What?" He scowled, meeting the man's disbelieving stare. "Allie was damn near killed three days ago while under their watch. You really think I'm just going to hand her back over to them and hope they do a better job of protecting her this time?"

"Hey, man. Whatever you say." His partner acted as if it wasn't any sweat off his back.

Sometimes the guy was a serious pain in his ass.

Between Noah's six-three muscular build and thick dark hair and beard—both with splatters of silver—it was no wonder the women in the office had dubbed him Denver's sexiest silver fox. Of course, for Noah, there was only one woman who mattered.

The same woman who'd taken Allie with her to get that coffee.

"You got something to say, just say it so we can move the fuck on," Wade growled.

Much too innocently, Noah asked, "Say what?"

"Whatever the hell it is you're *not* saying."

"It's nothing." His partner shrugged. "You just seem... different. That's all."

Wade looked back at the man as if he'd lost his mind. "Dude, you just saw me three days ago."

"So?"

"*So*, nothing's changed."

Bringing his fist to his mouth, Noah released a fake-as-fuck cough as he simultaneously said, "Bullshit."

"It's not bullshit!"

The other man propped himself on the edge of Wade's desk. With his voice lowered so the other agents around them couldn't hear, Noah said, "Look, man. I get it."

"Yeah?" Wade leaned back in his chair. "And what exactly is it you think you get?"

"You like her. And you want to be the one to protect her."

"I don't—"

"Save it, Crenshaw," Noah cut off the lie he was about to tell. "I saw the way you two were together when you first came in this morning. The way you look at her...how she looks at you. It's exactly how Maggie and I are with each other."

He's right. Wade knew the man was fucking right. He'd all but confessed his feelings for Allie on the sidewalk outside the diner the other day. So why was he having such a hard time admitting it to his best friend?

Because saying it out loud to someone else will make it real. And when things get real, he felt even more vulnerable.

When did I turn into such a coward?

"Fine." Wade finally admitted what he'd been holding back. "I like her, okay?"

Noah's lips twitched. "Oh, I'd say you more than like her."

"Jesus, man." He barely fought his own smile. "I told you how I was her protective detail back in Virginia, before the trial."

"Let me guess. That's when you two got…close."

"Yeah, but not like that." He glanced around to make sure no one was listening. "We both knew where it was headed, but I kept it professional until after the trial."

"And that's when you slept together?"

"What? No." Wade shook his head. "We never…we haven't…" He blew out a breath and ran a hand over the scruff on his jaw. "I mean, we would have, but the day of Costa's sentencing was the same day Allie's parents were murdered. We knew right away the bastard was behind it, and if he could get to her parents while behind bars, then—"

"They could get to her."

He nodded. "She was immediately put into WITSEC, and until three days ago, I hadn't seen or talked to her since."

"Damn. That's rough." Noah frowned. "It was hard enough going a few months without seeing Maggie before she came here from Dallas. I can't imagine having to go five *years* without her."

"Yeah, but you and Maggie are different."

"Are we?" His partner stared down at him knowingly. "Look, man. All I'm saying is, you got a second chance at life. Don't fuck it up by letting the one thing that makes you happy slip through your fingers."

Wade knew the man was right. He'd not only been given a second chance at life…he'd also been given a second chance at love.

Not that he was ready to hand in his man card and admit that just yet.

Scooting back up to his desk, he cleared his throat and picked up the file once more. "You gonna sit here playing couple's therapy all damn day, or are we actually going to get some work done to help solve this case?"

With another knowing grin, Noah stood and started for his desk, which was butted up against Wade's. "If it'll make you feel better, I'll text Mags and see what's taking them so long."

Right on cue, Allie and Maggie walked through the open doorway, each carrying two lidded to-go cups in their hands. Both standing just a little over five feet, the two women were both petite with curves in all the right places.

But contrary to Maggie's slightly tanned skin and dark curly hair, Allie was a bit paler with long blonde hair. And while Maggie was clearly an attractive woman, she didn't have the same primal effect on him that Allie always had.

Something Noah's wife said made Allie laugh, and damn if the sound wasn't the most beautiful thing he'd ever heard.

God, I've missed hearing that.

"We were about to send out the calvary to look for you two." Noah took the cup Maggie offered to him and planted a chaste kiss on her cheek.

The sweet woman smiled up at her husband as if he hung the moon. "The coffee shop was busy, so Allison and I used the time to get to know each other."

"Call me Allie." The woman Wade couldn't take his eyes from smiled. "That's what my friends call me."

She already considers Maggie a friend. That's good. Really fucking good.

Wade was struck with a sudden and fierce urge to pull her in his arms and claim her as his. If they were back at his apartment right now, he just might have. Because having her under his roof these past two nights and *not* doing all the things to her he wanted had been pure torture.

Having decided he didn't want to push her too far too fast, especially given the circumstances that had brought them back together, nothing more had happened between them since that day outside the diner.

Their first night in Denver, they were both so completely wiped from the drive, they'd crashed as soon as they'd gotten to his place. Her in his bed. Him on the couch.

Yesterday, they'd taken some time to catch up on some much-needed sleep. Once they woke up and showered—separately, of course—they'd spent the afternoon shopping for more clothes and necessities for her, as well as making a grocery run to fill his near-empty cupboards and fridge.

Between his hectic work schedule and living life as a single man, Wade tended to either grab something while he was out, or have food delivered once he was home.

He'd never really given that, or the appearance of his dull bachelor pad, much thought until Allie. But now...

Everything's different when it comes to her.

"Have you had any luck reaching John?" Her soft voice brought him back to the moment at hand.

"Thanks." Wade took the coffee she'd been kind enough to buy him. "Not yet. I've left at least ten messages, and now when I call, it says his voicemail is full."

The skin between her light brown brows bunched together. "I'm really starting to get worried."

Wade was starting to get pissed.

For the past three days, he and Allie had been trying to reach the man assigned as her handler by the U.S. Marshals. She'd tried his secure cell line, while Wade attempted to contact him through his office in Virginia. The bastard had yet to call either of them back.

Fucker better be dead.

Any other excuse for leaving a protected witness high and dry was unacceptable in Wade's eyes.

"The Marshals are probably all busy scrambling around, trying to figure out where the hell their witness ran off to." Noah looked at him expectantly.

The man hadn't hidden the fact that he thought Wade should just call the U.S. Marshal office right there in Denver. If for no other reason, than to at least let them know their witness was safe.

But if he did that, they'd either come straight here or wait for them to show back up at his apartment. Either way, there wasn't a chance in hell he was risking losing Allie again.

Not to them, or Costa's men.

"They nearly got her killed once already." He pointed out. "You really think I'm going to put her life in their hands again?" Inching closer to her, Wade made it crystal clear where he stood. "I'm not giving anyone jack shit until I know for sure who we can trust. And right now, the only people I trust are the ones standing in this room."

"I can't say I blame you, Wade." Maggie took his side.

"I don't either." Noah shook his head. "I just hate knowing there are government agents out there busting their asses to find her. That's all."

"And I get that. But how the hell do you think Costa's men figured out where she was living in the first place?"

The question made Allie frown. "You think someone in the Marshals office tipped them off?"

Wade met her ocean blue stare. "Don't you? Think

about, Al. They're the only people who knew where you'd been placed."

"It wasn't John." She sounded adamant about that. "He'd never risk my safety like that."

"Well, if it wasn't Napier, then it had to be someone else in that office."

"I agree." Noah joined in again. "Costa had to have gotten to one of them. Sure as hell wouldn't be the first time a mob boss had someone working for him on the inside."

"But why now?" Maggie asked. "You said this Costa guy went to prison five years ago. Why wait this long to go after Allie?"

Wade thought for a moment. "The transfer." He looked at Allie and the others. "He was biding his time until the perfect opportunity came along to escape."

Noah began shaking his head. "Yeah, but you know how guys like that work. He could've had her taken out years ago, even from the inside." As if realizing what he'd just said, he quickly turned to Allie and said, "Sorry. I didn't mean for that to sound so..."

"It's okay." She offered Noah a small smile. "I know what you meant. And I've been thinking about that."

"You have some thoughts?" Wade studied her closely.

She hesitated slightly, and then, "I think he wanted us to know it was him. Not that I've given anyone else a reason to want me dead," she chuckled nervously. "But I think...I think Costa is the kind of man who wouldn't want there to be a question as to who ordered those men to kill me."

"Like he's sending a message?" Maggie sounded intrigued.

Sliding a glance in Maggie's direction, Allie nodded. "One thing I learned about Costa during the trial, even when the judge was handing down his sentence, was that he likes for people to know he's in charge."

As Wade considered this, the pieces of her well-formulated puzzle clicked into place. "He waited until the day of his escape to put the hit out on you so everyone would know for sure it was him."

Not that there was ever any doubt.

"Makes sense," Noah agreed.

Wade brushed his hand against Allie's and smiled. "That's good. Smart."

The corners of her bow-shaped lips curved upward. "I know it doesn't really help much, but..."

"No, it does," he disagreed. "That's one less question we have to find the answer to."

"What's the next answer we need to find?" She stared up at him anxiously.

With a silent vow to do so, he told her, "Figuring out who gave up your location."

"Sounds like y'all have a lot of work to do, and so do I." Maggie rose onto her tiptoes and gave Noah a kiss on the lips. "I'll see you later."

"Love you," the man said without caring who heard him.

A slight blush creeped into Maggie's cheeks as she stared up at her husband with affection. "Love you, too." To Allie, she said, 'You need anything, don't hesitate to call. Even if it's just to plan another coffee date."

"I will." Allie smiled at her new friend. "Thanks, Maggie."

Noah watched his wife walk away, then turned back to Wade.

"Maggie told me how you two met," Allie shared. "Sounds like she was very lucky."

"Nah, I'm the lucky one." Noah's mouth turned up with a

half-smile. "It's amazing what a difference finding the right woman can do for a man." His dark gaze slid to Wade's and stayed there for a good, long second.

Way to be subtle, asshole.

Clearing his throat, Wade changed the subject back to work. "We need to find that leak. We find that person, we can start working our way up the chain. Hopefully get a bead on Costa's location."

"Well, you don't want to call the Marshals office directly, so... Is there anyone you know who might have an in?"

"I was hoping John Napier would call me back, but he seems to be ignoring our calls."

"Or is he?" Allie chimed in. Pulling her cardigan closed, she crossed her arms in front of her. "In the five years I've been in WITSEC, John has never *not* returned my calls."

Shit. He'd been so pre-occupied with bringing Allie here and trying to find a way to track down Costa and his men, he hadn't considered the possibility that Napier hadn't returned his call because he wasn't *able* to.

Wade's expression intensified. "You think something's happened to him?"

"I don't know. I mean, I hope so. But the more I think about it, the more worried I get thinking they may have used him to get to me." Her eyes glistened with unshed tears. "I know in my heart John would never willingly tell Costa or his men were I was, but what if..." She brought her watery gaze to his. "God, Wade. What if they did something to him? What if..." Allie swiped at a tear that had escaped. "What if he didn't have a choice but to tell them where I was?"

"We need to find John Napier," Noah stated the obvious. "*That* needs to be our next step."

He mulled over another way to find out where the man could be. "If I keep calling his office, they might suspect I know where Allie is. And since we don't know who leaked her assigned address in Texas, I'm not willing to risk exposing her to the wrong person."

The three of them stood near the pair of desks, each silently contemplating a way to find Napier without revealing where Allie was, now. Noah was the first to speak up.

"What about your old partner back in D.C.? What was his name..."

"Landry."

"He still connected to Costa's case?"

Wade nodded. "He took over after I left."

At the time, there wasn't anything to take over since Costa had just been handed down a life sentence. But since Wade was no longer with that division of the FBI, the reins had been handed down to his then-partner.

"You said before that you didn't trust anyone who wasn't in this room," Allie's voice quivered with her obvious efforts to keep her emotions at bay. "Don't you trust Agent Landry?"

Prior to his leaving, he and Ryan had been through hell and back together. Worked several hairy cases, and even a few high-profile ones. Including Costa's.

Ryan Landry was one of the best federal agents Wade had ever had the pleasure to work with. The guy was as solid as they came, and there was never a time when Wade had doubted the man's dedication to the job. Ryan always had his back without fail, and Wade had done the same for him.

He'd trusted the man with his life back then, and in his world, that meant one hell of a lot.

"Yeah, sweetheart." The endearment slipped out as Wade thumbed away another tear she didn't seem to notice.

"I do."

"While you call him, I'm going to go see if Michael's gotten around to pulling security cam footage from the businesses along Main Street in Salado."

Normally, Agent Michael Wright—the unit's lead technical analyst—worked from his own desk right there in the unit's designated space. But he'd been sent upstairs training the divisions tech group on a new system that had been installed at the end of last week.

Looking surprised by Noah's plan, Allie's focus shifted to Noah. "You can do that? Access a business's cameras, just like that?"

"If we get permission from the owners or a warrant. Thanks to Detective West, we were able to bypass the time it would take to contact the owners."

"How's that?" Wade wanted to know.

"Apparently, West's brother's boss has connections out the ass. Including a Judge in Bell County, where Salado happens to be."

"That's...wow." Allie blinked.

"Right?" Noah grinned as he began walking past. "Let's just hope the cameras picked up a good enough shot for facial rec."

Hell yeah, Wade was hoping for that. It was always good to know the faces and names of the men you intended to kill.

"Why don't you take a load off?" He pointed to Noah's chair. "Trust me, he won't mind."

Accepting the offer, Allie carried her coffee around to the other man's desk and sat down. She looked a bit better than yesterday, Wade noted. Her coloring held a little more pink than before, and with the extra sleep she'd been able to get at his place, the shadows beneath her eyes were less prominent.

I'll make them go away, baby. I swear, I'll do everything in my power to make sure you don't have another sleepless night again.

With Noah on his way to the building's third floor, Wade sat in his own chair and picked up his desk phone. Dialing the number he still knew by heart, he waited as the ringing began.

One ring. Two rings. Three rings...

"Landry."

Wade released a sigh of relief. "Hey, Ryan. It's Wade."

There was a slight pause and then, "Crenshaw? Hey, man! Long time no talk. How the hell are ya?"

It had been a long time since they'd taken the time to catch up. Too long.

"I'd be better if you could tell me Lorenzo Costa is back in federal custody."

"Heard about that, huh?" His ex-partner sighed. "Yeah, it's been a complete shitshow around here the last few days. We've got a BOLO going, put road blocks and checkpoints on every major road...hell, we've even started canvassing the rural areas nearby with abandoned barns and farmhomes."

"You pick up any leads?"

Ryan hesitated slightly, and Wade understood why. This wasn't his case. Not anymore.

"Between you and me?" The other man lowered his voice to a near-whisper. "We ain't got shit."

Damn it.

"I was afraid of that."

"Yeah, but don't worry. The guy's face is constantly being plastered anywhere and everywhere people will see it.

Mainstream media, social media, newspapers, billboards…you name it, we're doing it."

"Good to know."

"We'll get the bastard sooner or later, don't you worry. We've got everyone working this one, including local law enforcement across the state."

Nothing the man said was surprising. Costa wasn't the first time a federal prisoner had escaped custody, and unfortunately, he wouldn't be the last. His old unit knew how to take care of business, and from what Ryan had just told him, that was exactly what they were doing.

"That's good to hear, man," Wade told the other man. "I knew you'd be on top of things."

"Good, because for a minute there, I was beginning to think you'd lost faith in my abilities to take down pieces of shit like Costa."

"Never." He drew in a breath and got to the real reason for the call. "Hey, listen. I do have a favor to ask."

"And here I thought you called because you missed the sound of my sweet voice."

Wade chuckled. "Well, that goes without saying."

"All right, Crenshaw. Lay it on me."

"You remember John Napier? He's the U.S. Marshal who was put in charge of the witness after Costa's trial."

"Napier…Napier…" Ryan seemed to let the name roll through his memories. "Oh, yeah. Isn't he the guy who stole your girl from you?"

"He didn't steal…" Wade pressed his lips together. He didn't have time to waste arguing petty shit. "Sure. That guy."

"Whoa. You're not even going to deny it?"

"Ryan…" Wade's tone was full of warning.

"Okay, fine. Damn, man. I'm beginning to think all that high elevation stunted your sense of humor."

No, damn near losing the woman I plan to build a future with took care of that.

"Listen, I've been trying to get ahold of the guy for the past two days, but he's not answering his secured line or the one at his office, and he hasn't returned any of my calls."

"That's odd. You talk to his partner or anyone in his office? Maybe he's on vacation or home sick or something."

"I don't want to talk to anyone else but him."

"Okaaay... Any particular reason why?"

He needed to be very careful, here. "Nothing I can talk about on this phone."

"Ooh. How very cloak-and-dagger of you."

"I'm serious, Ryan. This is important."

Several seconds passed before his ex-partner finally got serious. "Okay, man. Whatever you say." Another pause and then, "Wait a minute. This isn't about the girl, is it? I mean, you don't think Costa would be stupid enough to go after her right away, do you?"

"He already did," Wade revealed. "Thankfully, she got away, but barely."

"So you're what, trying to find Napier so you can let him know? Because I'm sure he and the Marshals have already—"

"I'm trying to find out who the fuck gave Costa her information," Wade spat out.

Every time he thought about the danger Allie had been placed in, the angrier he got.

Like before, there was a long moment before Ryan spoke again. "You think Napier's dirty?"

"I don't know what I think, but I *won't* know until I talk to the man myself."

"And you don't want to tip off the other Marshals in case it's not him."

"Exactly." Wade nodded. "The men who found Allie were definitely Costa's, and the only way that happens is if someone tipped them off. If it's not Napier, then it has to be someone in that office."

"All right, man." Ryan agreed. "I've got a contact there who owes me a favor. If anyone can find out what's up with Napier, it's her."

"Don't tell her why you're asking, though."

"Seriously, Crenshaw? You act like this is my first rodeo." Ryan sounded insulted. "Relax, okay? No one will know I've even spoken to you. I'll just make it seem like I need to talk to Napier about the situation with Costa. As the lead on the case, no one would think anything of it."

Which is exactly why I called you.

"Thanks, brother." Wade's tense muscles relaxed.

"There is one condition, though."

Ryan used to love making deals. Apparently, some things never changed. "What's that?"

"You gotta promise you'll come back to D.C. for a visit. Soon. Wizards games just aren't the same without ya."

Wade smiled. "Deal."

"Give me a few minutes, and I'll call you back."

"Appreciate it."

"Hey, what are ex-partners for?"

Wade ended the call and found Allie staring back at him expectantly. "Well?"

"They have no leads on Costa, but they've got everyone out there looking for him."

"And John?"

"Ryan's going to see what he can find out and call me back."

She blew out a breath and settled back in Noah's chair. "I just hope John's all right."

"I'm sure he's fine," Wade did his best to reassure her. "Like Noah said, John's office is probably busy trying to find you."

Except, as her handler, the first thing Napier should've done was try to contact Allie. The fact that he'd gone radio silent at the exact same time two men broke into her apartment with the intent to kill her…yeah, that shit didn't bode well for the man.

Not that he was about to tell her that.

For the next several minutes, Wade did everything he could to try to distract Allie from thinking the worst. He asked about her time with Maggie down at the building's coffee shop, what she wanted for dinner…anything and everything to keep her mind off the news they were waiting to hear.

Then they got the call.

"Crenshaw."

"It's me."

"What did you find out?"

"It's not good, man."

Schooling his expression to keep from upsetting Allie, Wade said, "Tell me."

"John Napier's body was discovered about an hour ago. Apparently, some teenagers who decided to go exploring found him down in the Dupont Underground."

The Dupont Underground was a series of old abandoned Trolley tunnels located a mile away from the White House.

"Anything else?" He chose his words carefully, because he wanted to give Allie the news in private, rather than surrounded by a bunch of men and women she didn't know.

"Cause of death is going to take some time." Ryan waited a beat and then, "The guy was tortured, Wade. As in bones broken and fingers cut off kind of torture. So I'd say he's your leak."

Sonofabitch.

"Thanks, Ryan. You find anything else out, you'll keep me in the loop, yeah?"

"Of course. Wish I had better news."

"It's okay." It really wasn't. "We'll talk soon."

Hanging up the phone, Wade took half a second before lifting his gaze to Allie's.

"Well? Did he find John?"

He stood and walked over to her. With his hand held out, he said, "Let's go talk somewhere else."

"No." Allie stood without his help. "Just tell me."

"Allie, I really think we should—"

"Damn it, Wade. John isn't just my handler. He's also my friend. So please, whatever you have to say, just say it."

A few of the other agents looked their way, but when they made eye contact with Wade, they quickly went back to whatever they were doing before.

I'm so sorry, sweetheart.

"John is dead." He lowered his hand. "They found his body an hour ago."

Allie's head swiveled back and forth with denial. "No."

"I'm sorry, Al."

"Oh, my God." She fell back into the seat. With new tears falling as quickly as she wipe the old ones away, she said, "How?"

"You don't need to hear the details."

"Don't tell me what I need or don't need. I've managed to take care of myself for this long. I can handle whatever it is you aren't saying."

Damn. He always did have a habit of underestimating her strength.

"Okay." Wade squatted down beside her. Needing her to know he was there for her, he covered her hand with his and told her the truth. "Allie, John was tortured to death."

Her bottom lip quivered, her eyes filling with sorrow for the man she'd clearly grown to care about. "And you think he told them where to find me?"

"I do." Noah nodded. "The things that were done to him...baby, I know John was a good Marshal and a good friend. But a man can only take so much before he breaks."

Using her free hand, Allie reached up and dried the tears from her cheeks. "So what now? You and Noah, you said the first thing was to find John, and now you have. Plus, if he's the one who gave me up, then that question has been answered, too. So what's our next step?"

Jesus, she was amazing. Her world had been turned upside down. Again. But instead of breaking down into a complete mess--which would be totally understandable, given her situation—she was already trying to figure out their next move.

"For now, I'm going to take you back to my place until I can find out more."

"I don't need to be handled, Wade."

"Not trying to handle you, sweetheart. As much as I hate to admit it, I'm at a standstill as far as Costa is concerned."

"What about Noah?" She sniffled. "Won't he be expecting us to be here when he gets back?"

"I'll text him and let him know where we'll be. If he finds out anything more, he can email it to me or bring it by my place."

He could tell she wanted to argue, but thankfully Allie gave in without much of a fight. Standing, Wade moved back to give her space, but not too much. He reached for her, his chest warming when she put her small hand in his.

And as he led her past the other agents in the room and into the small hallway leading to the elevators, Wade started to plan.

First, he was going to get her home so she could grieve for her friend in private. After that...

He was going to use every resource he had—including one he already owed—to do whatever it took to end this. Wade didn't care what he had to do, he'd turn over every fucking rock between here and Virginia if it meant finding that murdering bastard, Costa.

And then, once the threats to Allie's safety had been eliminated, he was going to do what he'd wanted since the night they first met.

He was going to make her his.

6

Allison stared at herself in the bathroom mirror. The steam had dissipated long ago and yet, here she still stood. Staring at a woman she barely recognized.

Thick, damp strands of her long blonde hair hung over her bare shoulders like a sporadic waterfall. Her eyes—still puffy and red from her earlier crying jag in the shower—were filled with the sorrow and pain she felt for her friend.

I'm so sorry, John.

From their many talks over the years, Allison knew the kind Marshal had left behind a wife, two grown daughters, and five grandchildren. Her heart physically hurt with the knowledge that two of those babies were only months old and would never know just how much their grandpa loved them.

She didn't blame him for telling whoever tortured him where she was. Like Wade said, a man could only withstand so much pain before he broke. Even one as dedicated and strong as John Napier.

Her mind conjured up a horrific image of the man.

Though she fought against it, Allison pictured him bloody and beaten. Or worse.

Wade had spared her the details of what they'd done to John, and for that, she was grateful. But sometimes, the things her mind imagined could be worse than reality.

A tear escaped the corner of her eye, but she swatted it away before it could fall. God, she was so *sick* of this.

The senseless violence and bloodshed. The terror one man had created, simply because he could. And for what purpose?

Lorenzo Costa was a free man, now. A fugitive from justice, yes, but still. With the resources he still had, the guy could fly off to some non-extraditable country somewhere and live out the rest of his days in the sand and sun.

So why waste his newfound freedom going after her? There was only one answer Allison could think of.

Because he can.

"Hey, Allie?" Wade's gentle tone was joined by a soft knock on the door. "You all right in there?"

No. "Yeah, I'm good. I'm about done."

"Okay. I just wanted to let you know I made us some food. No rush, though."

The aching in her heart eased slightly. Then again, Wade had always had that effect on her.

"Thanks." Her voice came out a bit stronger. "I'll be out in just a second."

"Take your time."

She waited until she heard him walk away before reaching for the doorknob. When they'd gotten back to his apartment, she hadn't put much thought about what she was doing. Only that she didn't want to break down into a blubbering mess in front of him.

So she'd walked straight back to the bathroom

connected to his bedroom, stripped herself down, and let the shower's hot water wash away her tears. It wasn't until now that she realized the clothes she'd planned to change into were still in the bag at the corner of his room.

With one of Wade's large, terrycloth towels wrapped snuggly around her body, Allison opened the door and peeked outside. As she'd suspected, he'd shut his bedroom door behind him when he left.

Not that the idea of being naked with the sexy man hadn't ever crossed her mind. To the contrary, there had been many, many nights she'd fantasized about what it would be like to feel his strong hands on her bare skin.

And she didn't mean just holding hands.

The few kisses they'd shared since that first one a few days ago had been perfect and sweet. But then reality kicked in, and they'd both been too focused on finding Costa to give much thought as to what it all meant.

Once this mess was over and her enemies were back behind bars where they belonged, Allison hoped they'd continue exploring a future she'd prayed to find. A future that included her, Wade, and a lifetime of happiness.

Stepping out into the bedroom, she was bent over grabbing the plastic bag her new things were still in when she heard the bedroom door open behind her. With a tiny squeal, she shot up and spun around, a few strands of her damp hair sticking to her flushed cheek in the process.

Standing halfway in the doorway looking as mouthwatering as usual, Wade had changed out of his suit and tie, and into a pair of faded jeans and a black tee. Of course, the man could be wearing a feed sack and he'd still push all her girly buttons.

"Sorry." He was quick to apologize. "I thought you were still in the bathroom."

"It's okay."

Though she could tell he was trying to hide it, Allison didn't miss the way his eyes wandered down the length of her body. Nor did she miss the heat flaming behind his fiery gaze when his gray eyes rose back up to meet hers.

"I, uh…I made spaghetti, and couldn't remember if you liked meat with your sauce."

"I like meat." She nodded, praying he didn't take her response as a double entendre.

You sure you didn't mean it to be one?

"Great. I'll add it to the sauce."

"Sounds good."

The awkward conversation seemed to have ended, yet Wade stood there for another long moment before he cleared his throat and tore his gaze from hers. "Okay, then. I'll get the table set. Just come whenever you're ready."

"Okay." Allison offered him a smile.

"Okay."

Blinking, Wade turned away, shutting the door once more as he left. Allison released a breath she hadn't realized she'd been holding and grabbed the bag from the floor, carrying it over to the bed.

After donning the new bra and panty set she'd bought, she decided to go with comfort over style. Dressing in a pair of dark gray leggings and a lavender hoodie, she went back into the bathroom to run a brush through her tangled hair.

Her stomach growled, reminding her it had been several hours since she'd eaten. Wade had whipped up some bacon, scrambled eggs, and toast before they left for the Bureau this morning, and though he'd offered several times to get her something for lunch, she hadn't been even slightly hungry then.

Not surprising, given the fact that a typical breakfast for her was a cup of coffee and a granola bar.

Now that she'd had a good, long cry, Allison found herself surprisingly famished. And from the delicious aromas traveling through the apartment, she was going to enjoy Wade's spaghetti dinner immensely.

Setting the brush down onto the vanity, she walked barefoot across the cool wooden floor to the kitchen. When she got there, she found Wade carrying a big bowl of prepared Caesar salad over to the small, square table.

In a gentlemanly move, he pulled out a chair for her and smiled. "It's nothing fancy, but hopefully it tastes all right."

"This looks amazing, Wade." Allison sat down. "Thank you."

"There's garlic bread in the oven, but it's not quite done yet." He chose the seat across from her.

"You didn't have to do all of this."

"It's spaghetti, Al. Not prime rib."

"I know." She chuckled softly as she placed a scoop of salad onto her plate. "I just feel like all you ever do is take care of me."

"I like taking care of you."

The low rumble of his voice had her looking up, and the raw heat she found in his eyes as they stared back into hers nearly left her gasping.

Oh, yeah. He definitely wants you.

The realization shouldn't be a surprise. He'd already told her as much that day on the sidewalk. But a part of her —the part that remembered how heartbreaking it was when she thought he hadn't contacted her because he didn't care —was still threatening to put a cloud over his claim.

I like taking care of you.

Hearing those words now combined with the way he

was looking at her...Allison had little doubt that the man meant everything he'd ever said to her. Yes, it hurt when she thought he'd forgotten about her, but his explanation as to why he hadn't called or texted was more than a little believable.

He hadn't written her off and moved on with his life because he didn't care. Wade had simply been doing what he'd always done. He'd been protecting her.

Just like he's protecting me, now.

"Taste okay?"

Allison shook away her thoughts and brought herself back into the moment. "It's great. Thanks again for doing all of this."

"Well, I don't claim to be the best chef in the world, but it's kind of hard to screw up spaghetti."

Smiling, she shook her head. "I didn't only mean the meal. I meant for everything."

"I haven't really done much." Wade shrugged it off.

"You've put your life on hold to come get me. You've bought me clothes, practically moved me into your apartment...you even convinced your boss to allow you to use company time and resources to help me." Allison drew in a breath and let it out slowly. "I guess what I'm trying to say is thank you. I know it's not enough, and I'll never be able to repay what I owe you, but...I hope it's at least a start."

Placing his fork on the edge of his plate, Wade leaned his elbows on the table and locked his intense gaze with hers. "Let's get something clear right now. You don't owe me a damn thing. If anything, I'm the one who owes you."

"You?" She stared back at him as if he'd lost his mind. "How do you figure that?"

"You wouldn't even be in this mess if I hadn't pushed you to testify against Costa."

"No, I'd be dead."

Her words seemed to spark something inside him. Something dark and angry. "Don't say that."

"Why not? It's the truth."

Suddenly losing her appetite, Allison pushed her chair out and stood. Walking aimlessly into the living room, she stopped in front of the gas fireplace and wrapped her arms around herself.

"I used to blame you." She turned her head to see Wade slowly walking toward her. "For a really long time, I blamed you for everything. My parents' deaths...my having to live a life that wasn't really mine...I put all of it on you because it was easier than facing the truth."

"What truth is that?" He came to stand directly in front of her.

"The truth is, everything that happened is my fault."

"Allie, no..."

"I don't mean Rick's murder. Just the fact that I was there when it happened. If I'd gone home that night when Rick first told me to, I never would have been in that alley, and I never would've seen Lorenzo Costa's or Eddie Veneto's faces. But I ignored Rick when he told me to leave, and because of that, I put into play a chain of events so horrific that most days, I can't even look at myself in the mirror."

"Ah, sweetheart." Wade took the side of her face into his palm. "There's not a damn thing about this mess that's your fault."

"Did you not just hear what I said?"

"I heard you." He nodded his handsome head. "And what I heard...*all* I heard...was that you were a sweet, caring young woman who didn't want to leave her boss to have to deal with all the mess and clean-up alone."

"That's not the point."

"That's exactly the point. You stayed behind to help because that's the kind of person you are. Costa and his goon showing up was just a matter of being in the wrong place at the wrong time. Not to mention, think of all the lives that have been saved these last five years *because* you were there to I.D. him."

She hadn't really thought of it that way before.

"Maybe, but—"

"There's no maybe to it." With his other hand, he framed her face completely. "Lorenzo Costa is a ruthless son of a bitch who was off the streets and behind bars for over half a decade. *You* did that." He leaned in and brushed his lips against hers. "Your strength and bravery did that."

"What if we can't catch him again?" She stared up into Wade's slate-colored eyes, desperate for some piece of security to hold onto. *Anything* that would tell her they would catch the man who was truly responsible.

"We will." He kissed her again. "I promise you, we will."

"Together?" She had to know. Because this time, she wasn't about to be hidden away like some deep dark secret.

"You and me."

Allison wasn't sure who moved first. All she did know was that one minute she was lost in his mesmerizing stare, and the next they were devouring each other in the middle of his living room.

She tore at the hem of his shirt until he broke free long enough to pull it up over his head. Wade yanked her hoodie off and tossed it aside—where it landed, she didn't know. And didn't care.

Their mouths clashed together in a desperate mixture of tongues and heat. Devouring didn't even begin to describe the way they were attacking each other. He gave, she took. He licked, she nibbled.

The aching need Allison felt in her core was unlike anything she'd ever felt before. It was like a fire that continued to grow, its flames growing higher and higher with every second that passed.

And the only hope of extinguishing it was the man currently lifting her in his arms.

"Couch or bed?" he growled. His hands gripped the curves of her ass as he started to walk.

Wrapping her arms around his neck, Allison told him, "Couch," and held on tight. After all this time, she couldn't believe this was finally happening.

Sure, the timing wasn't ideal. Far from it. But she'd spent so much of her adult life focused on death and dying, it was time she started *living*.

And what better way to start than making love to the only man she'd ever truly wanted?

They reached the couch. Wade released his hold and carefully guided her down the length of his body. His hands went to her waistband. Hers went for his belt.

Within seconds, she'd shoved his jeans and boxers down his toned legs, and he'd removed her lacey bra and panties.

The grays in Wade's eyes darkened to a smokey slate as he took in her naked form. "Jesus," he panted. "You're so fucking beautiful."

Allison should probably feel embarrassed from being so exposed, but she wasn't. Being with Wade, like this, seemed incredibly...right.

"So are you." She inched forward. Tearing her gaze from his, she let herself look at him for the very first time.

His broad shoulders and muscular chest came as no surprise. Back when she was under his protection the first time, Allison had spent many an evening sneaking whatever glimpses she could.

But studying the way his dress shirts and tees stretched across his masculine form was nothing compared to seeing him stripped bare.

Every dip and shadow. Every curve and smooth line. The way his torso narrowed with the six pack he obviously worked hard to maintain... And the sharp V leading down to the impressive erection jutting out between his thick thighs...

Lord have mercy!

The man was male perfection at its finest. And, at least for the moment, he was all hers.

Something caught her eye, drawing her focus to the lower left side of Wade's abs.

"What happened here?" She ran her fingertips across a small, circular area of puckered skin there.

"I was shot while on duty a few months back."

Her eyes flew to his. Tears threatened to form at the thought of him lying on the ground, in pain and bleeding.

He could've died. He could've died and I wouldn't have known.

Not until it was too late.

"I'm okay, Al," he rasped. "Docs patched me up, and I'm good as new."

She studied him closely for any signs he might be lying. But all she found in his peering eyes was a wanton need... and an emotion she didn't dare try to name.

Putting all thoughts of gunshots and dying out of her head, Allison reached out and took him in her fist. Wade hissed in sharp a breath, an instant reaction from her touch.

It only encouraged her more.

She began pumping him up and down slowly, enjoying the feeling of steel covered in velvet beneath her palm. He pulsed beneath her touch, but when she ran her thumb over the damp, swollen tip, Wade pulled her hand free and grabbed hold of her hips.

"What are you—"

"Sweetheart, you keep doing that, this'll all be over before we even get started."

With a sly smirk, Allison raised a brow and said, "Then I guess we'd better get to it."

Humor mixed with arousal as Wade lifted her up and spun them around. Sitting on the couch behind him, he positioned them so she was straddling him. Her heated, damp core rubbing against the solid shaft she'd held in her hand mere seconds ago.

"You sure about this?"

Allison nearly smiled at the adorably nervous expression. Did he really think she was going to change her mind *now*?

Not a chance in hell.

She needed this. Needed *him*.

Sucky timing or not, it no longer seemed to matter. Life was short—something she knew better than most. So yeah, she was sure.

Rather than using her words to let him know, Allison lifted herself up onto her knees. Reaching between them, she positioned his body to hers, and with her eyes locked with his, she began to slowly lower herself onto him.

Wade groaned as she took him in. Inch by glorious inch, he stretched her body in ways it had never felt before. He was larger than her past lovers, not that she'd had many. Less than a handful, and those had all been before that fateful night so many years before.

Fully seated in her now, Allison took a moment to allow her sex to adjust. She'd never felt so full before. She'd never felt so *complete*.

Only him. Only with Wade.

"Jesus, you feel so good," he rumbled. His voice was deep and gravely, almost strained with his apparent effort to remain in control.

Allison leaned forward and kissed him. "So do you. I've wanted this for so long."

"Me too, sweetheart." He nibbled her bottom lip. "From the second we met.'

The admission left her pulse racing and her body begging for more. All this time, she had no idea he felt the same incredible pull toward her as she had him.

He felt it, too.

With renewed confidence and a sense of belonging, Allison began to move. She grabbed onto his shoulders as she rode him the way she'd always imagined.

Up. Down. Up. Down.

Wade held onto her hips as they gyrated back and forth. She moved slowly at first, and soon their bodies were working together in the most sensual of dances.

Their breathing picked up as they began to move faster. His hips thrust against hers as if they were keeping in time with the beat of their own glorious symphony.

Allison grabbed the back of the couch for better leverage. Her breaths sawed in and out as Wade's body filled hers with perfection.

Maybe because it *was* perfect. She and Wade fit together as if they were *made* for each other, and as she continued driving them toward a euphoric release, Allison began to think maybe…just maybe…they were.

"Shit, Al. I'm almost…there," Wade panted between thrusts. "Need you…to…come."

Before she could take matters into her own hands, he reached between them and expertly began rubbing her swollen clit. She was drenched with arousal, and the way he was playing her body...

"Mmmm," she groaned. Her eyes fell shut and she let her head fall backward. Giving herself over to this man was one of the easiest things she'd ever done.

"Oh, yeah. Just like that." She continued sliding up and down his body.

Harder.

Faster.

Her breasts bounced with every jolt, her body feeling even more alive when Wade reached up and filled his free hand with one of the perky globes. He kneaded her gently before taking her nipple between his thumb and forefinger.

Rubbing the distended nub, he sent an electric pulse racing toward the swollen bundle of nerves he was still praising.

"Oh, God, Wade." The telltale signs of her impending orgasm began rushing up her spine. "I'm almost there."

He moved his fingers faster. Pressed on her clit a little bit harder. And then...

"Oh, God...*Wade!*"

Allison cried out his name as an explosion of lights flashed behind her eyes. Every color, brighter than she'd ever seen them filled her vision as she was struck with the strongest, most intense climax of her existence.

Wade took over then, his body moving beneath hers to draw out her pleasure and bring him to the brink of his own.

His hands slid back to her hips. His muscles stiffened and his body jerked. Allison opened her eyes, unwilling to miss seeing this man reach the ultimate physical pleasure. Especially since she was the one who'd brought him there.

Seconds later, Wade was growling her name as his own

orgasm struck with a vengeance. Almost blindly, he pulled her close, his mouth slamming against hers, and together, they gave each other that last moment of carnal bliss.

She wasn't sure how long they sat like that... His lips on her lips, his body still inside hers. But as their beating hearts returned to a more normal pace, and the sensual fog began to clear, Allison became certain of one thing...

She loved this man. Heart and soul, crazy mobsters aside...he was it for her. And whether he realized it or not, she was his.

7

WADE WOKE with a smile on his face and the woman of his dreams snuggled up against his side. The morning sun was peeking through his curtains, and there was a cool breeze blowing through his bedroom window.

It took him a second to remember why he'd gone to bed with his window open. When he did, his smile grew even wider.

A few minutes after their mind-blowing sex on the couch, his smoke detectors had started going off, and his kitchen had filled with smoke. Apparently, garlic bread had a tendency to burn when it was left in the oven twenty minutes past the suggested baking time.

Oops.

He'd never seen Allie laugh as hard as she had in that moment. While he was battling the smoke and the alarm's piercing scream, Wade had decided on his new life goal.

To make her laugh like that every chance he got.

She shifted against him, her leg sliding over the top of his. Wade's heart did a funny sort of flip inside his chest, but he didn't question it or the overwhelming emotions that had finally filled his empty heart.

So this is what Noah was talking about.

Once his partner found out he was head over ass in love, Wade knew he'd have to listen to the I-told-you-so's. But he'd listen to Noah spout that shit all day long if it meant waking up to Allie's gorgeous face every morning.

A soft sigh reached his ears, and he looked down at her sleeping face. He lost his breath damn near every time he saw her, but fuck if she wasn't even more beautiful lying beside him in his bed.

After two rounds of the best sex he'd ever had—the one on his couch before he almost burned the place down, and the other in here, after they'd showered the smell of smoke from their hair—they'd heated up the spaghetti and cleaned up the mess before falling asleep in each other's arms.

His phone dinged from its place on his nightstand, alerting him of a new text. Reaching over, Wade grabbed it and opened the message from Noah.

You alive, or do I need to send the calvary?

Glancing at the clock, he was surprised to see it was after nine o'clock. Messaging him back, Wade wrote...

Here. Late night. Getting up now.

There was a pause before three tiny dots appeared, letting him know his partner was responding.

Bring Allie with you. Got footage from security cams. Angle doesn't show everything we need but I got a copy of the file on Costa and his men. Hoping she can make positive ID.

Back to reality they went.

Be there in thirty.

Returning the phone to his nightstand, Wade rolled over to wake Allie up. He was surprised to find her already staring back at him.

"Hey."

"Hey, yourself." She gave him a lazy smile. "For a second there, I thought last night was just a dream."

"Not a dream, sweetheart." He kissed her forehead, running his fingers up and down her bare hip. "I was about to wake you."

She pushed herself up on one elbow. Brushing some hair from her eyes, she asked, "Was that Noah? Did he find out anything more about John or Costa?"

He really hated disappointing her, but he wasn't about to lie. "Not yet. But he did get the security footage from the cameras in Salado. He wants me to bring you to the office so you can verify the men who came to your apartment."

"Okay." She frowned. "But they should be pretty easy to spot. Not like there are a lot of guys that go around shooting up Main Street."

"I know." He chuckled. "But apparently the camera's angle didn't get a good image, so he's going to have you look at some pictures. Hopefully, you recognize the man who shot you. If you can, that will give the asshole's defense attorney less chance of finding a loophole and getting these guys off on a technicality."

If it was up to him, these guys would never see the inside of a courtroom. However, Wade wasn't a murderer. That was Lorenzo Costa. But if he's ever given just cause, he wouldn't hesitate to kill each and every one of the bastards.

"Give me ten minutes, and I'll be ready."

Wrapping the sheet around her luscious body, he watched as Allie slid out of bed. Using it as a shield, she shuffled around the foot of the bed, grabbed her bag, and disappeared into the bathroom.

Wade smiled. He'd seen damn near every inch of her last night, yet here she was, acting all shy.

Goddamn, she's adorable.

Settling back onto his pillow, replaying the previous night's events. Making love to her still seemed like a dream, but he was thankful as fuck it wasn't.

Because reality was a thousand times better than his fantasies ever were.

As much as he hated to, Wade tossed off his comforter and padded across the room to his dresser. Normally, he liked to shower before work, but since he'd already done so right before they fell asleep, he felt okay about skipping it this time.

By the time Allie was out of the bathroom, he was dressed in his go-to FBI attire: Black dress pants, belt, and shoes, white button-up, a black blazer, and a tie.

And of course, his holster and standard department-issued Glock 19m.

Typically, Wade didn't pay much attention to the color of his ties, but today he decided to go with yellow. Yellow was a happy color, right? And right now, he felt like the happiest —and luckiest—fucker in the world.

"Mmm...suit porn." Allie strode over to him with a sly grin. She looked him up and down as if she were already contemplating round three.

Lord knows, I am.

Wait. Did she just say...

"Suit porn?"

"Oh, yeah." She nodded. "You know, sexy man. Sexy suit."

Ah, suit porn. Who knew?

"Well, you don't look too bad yourself."

She released a disbelieving scoff. "I'm in jeans and a sweater."

"So that would be, what? Jweater porn?" he teased. "Or would it be swean porn?"

Throwing her head back, Allie belted out a laugh that was instantly contagious. "I forgot how funny you were."

"Really?" He pulled her close. "'Cause there's not a damn thing about you I've forgotten."

Her expression softened. "This is crazy."

"What's that?"

"This." She motioned back and forth between them. "Us."

His gut tightened with fear that she was starting to regret what had happened between them. "I don't know. Doesn't seem so crazy to me."

"I don't mean us, just that..." Allie exhaled slowly. "Back in Virginia, the entire time you were protecting me, I wished something like this would happen. Then that day, right after the trial, there was a moment when it seemed like it might. But then—"

"Your world came crashing down."

She nodded. "I left and you stayed. Eventually, I gave up any hope that I'd ever see you again, let alone..."

"Have crazy monkey sex twice in one night?"

She burst out laughing. "Monkey sex?"

"Isn't that what the kids are calling it these days?"

Her eyes twinkled with humor. "I don't think so. But whatever you want to name it, it was incredible."

"It really was." Wade kissed the tip of her nose and then

her lips. She tasted minty, like his toothpaste. "So no regrets?"

"Not a single one." She didn't hesitate in the slightest, which made his heart swell. "You?"

"Fuck no." He frowned. "Well, I guess I do have one."

A sliver of fear flickered behind her round eyes. "What's that?"

He leaned in and began kissing the soft curve of her jaw and neck. "Only that we didn't do it sooner."

Allie let out a tiny sigh, her body melting against his. "You sure we have to go into the office today? Maybe we could take one more day to shut out the rest of the world." She moaned as he made his way to the other side of her neck. "You know, forget about the fact that there are men out there trying to kill me."

Her words were like a splash of cold water to his face. For a moment, he *had* forgotten that shit, and that was a very dangerous mistake to make.

"I'd love to, but the sooner we catch these guys, the sooner we can spend more days doing this."

Wade felt more than he saw her shoulders fall. But then, just like the strong woman he knew she was, Allie pulled out of his arms and straightened her spine.

"Then I guess we should go do whatever we need to do so we can get back to...this."

"Sweetheart, I love the way you think."

With a wink, Wade led them through the apartment and out the door. Keeping his head on a swivel, he was on constant alert as they made their way across the building's secured parking lot to where his black Dodge Charger was parked.

Twenty minutes later—after making a quick run through the Starbucks drive-thru for some coffee and bagels

—they were back on the Denver division's second floor. While Allie used the restroom, he went ahead and made his way over to his and Noah's desks.

"Morning." Sitting in his assigned seat, Noah greeted him with a jut of his chin. Looking behind him, he asked, "Where's Allie?"

"Bathroom. She'll be here in a sec."

Wade hated having her out of his sight for even a minute, but the restrooms were right across from the elevators, which were within his line of sight.

"Nice of you to finally grace us with your presence," his partner teased.

"Bite me, Killion." Wade's words held no heat. "Told you…long night."

Noah's dark eyes slid to where the restrooms were and back to Wade's. With a twitch of his lips, he said, "That so?"

"And that's the last comment like that you're going to make," Wade warned.

Sitting back into his chair, Noah's twitch turned into a full-grown smile. "Well, I'll be damned. Good for you."

"Dude. What part of 'last comment like that' was confusing for you? And so help me, you say a fucking word to Allie…"

"Oh, come on." Noah scooted back up and shook his head. "You really think I'd do that to her?"

No, he supposed Noah wouldn't. He was too classy for that shit. But even so…

"Well, don't. 'Cause she's dealing with enough shit. The last thing she needs is to feel self-conscious about what happened between us, too."

One of Noah's dark brows arched high. "Guess that answers that question."

Fuck me. You walked right into that one, didn't you, Crenshaw?

"Look, just promise me you're not going to say anything around her."

Noah grabbed a thick file from the side of his desk. "One last thing, and then my lips are sealed."

Sitting down at his own desk, Wade held back a frustrated growl and met his partner's serious gaze. "What?"

"I'm happy for you."

That wasn't what he expected. "Thanks."

"You're welcome. And by the way, here she comes."

On reflex, Wade turned to see Allie walking toward them. His chest warmed and the crotch of his pants tightened.

He didn't care what she'd said earlier. As far as he was concerned, the jeans-and-sweater look she had going on may as well be crotchless, see-through lacey lingerie. Clothes or no clothes, the woman made his dick stand up at attention every time she walked into the fucking room.

Noah greeted her with a smile. "Hey, Allie. How you doin' this morning?"

"Good." She slid a quick glance at Wade then back to Noah. "I'm good."

"That's great." Noah acted completely normal as he picked up the thick file. "Guess we should probably get started."

"Wade said something about a video and pictures..."

"Yeah. Wade said you two didn't have a chance to look at his email, so if you two want to come around here, we'll start with the images Agent Wright sent last night."

Wade stood, and he and Allie went over to stand on either side of Noah.

"Only one of the stores in Salado had their security cams angled so they could pick up who we believe to be the two men who shot at you."

Noah clicked a few buttons on his computer and an image popped up on his screen. He clicked 'play' and the video started.

In it, they could see two men park their car against a curb and get out. One was tall and thin, the other shorter and stockier. Though the image was blurry, Wade instinctively knew these were the guys.

Still, he looked at Allie and asked, "Are these the two men you saw?"

"That's them." She nodded, then pointed to the shorter of the two. "That's the one who shot me."

Wade's fists clenched at his sides. He wanted the man's name. His address. He wanted the man's *mother's* address... anything that would lead them to where the son of a bitch was.

"Okay, good." Noah nodded. "That's really good." He grabbed the thick file and opened it. "It took a bit, but Hunt was able to pull some strings and got a copy of the original case file on Costa from the D.C. office." To Wade, he added, "This stuff will probably look familiar to you, since you were the lead agent on that case."

Special Agent in Charge, or SAC Hunt was their direct supervisor. The man was tough as nails, but a damn good agent and even better boss.

Glancing at the folder's contents—or what he could see of it—Wade absolutely recognized it. He'd studied it front and back for months when he was still working in D.C.

Spreading several colored copies of what were originally five-by-seven photographs across the top of his desk, Noah looked up at Allie. "I need you to look at these men, and let me know if you recognize any of them."

Wade sure as hell did. Every man in those photos was connected to Lorenzo Costa in one way or another. Most were his minions. Lackeys who kept their mouths shut and blindly followed the mob boss's orders.

To start, Noah laid out six photos. Allie looked at each of them carefully, but when she got to the last one in that group, she shook her head. "None of these are the men I saw."

"Okay." Noah scooped them up and set them aside before laying out another six. "What about these? Any of those faces ring a bell?"

Wade watched as she studied each one closely. When she got to picture number four, she picked it up and looked over at him.

"This one." She handed the picture to Wade. "He was the taller one. The one driving the car."

Wade looked at the name and date of birth printed at the bottom of the photo. "Vinnie Markell," he uttered the man's name out loud. "I remember this guy. Used to be a small-time drug dealer before he joined Costa's crew. Worked his way up to being one of the bastard's main strong-arms." He lifted his gaze and looked at Allie and Noah. "If the boss needed someone to collect payments, Markell was one of his go-to men."

"Makes sense why Costa trusted him to take care of this job, then."

Yeah. It fucking did.

"Any of the rest of these look familiar to you, Allie?" Noah motioned toward the remaining five photos.

"No." She shook her head. "The other man isn't there."

"No problem." Like before, Noah picked up the photos and pulled out six more. "No problem. I've got one more stack."

"Jeez." Allie frowned. "How many guys does Costa have working for him?"

"Probably more than even we know about," Wade answered honestly.

Blinking, she blew out a breath and looked at the remaining six men. It took her all of two seconds to point out one of them as the shooter.

"Him!" she blurted excitedly. "He's the one who shot me."

"You're sure?"

"One hundred percent." Allie glanced over at Wade. "I'll never forget his face."

"Tony Antonelli," Wade said the name without bothering to look at the bottom of the man's picture. It was a face *he* wouldn't forget, either.

"You have a run-in with this one?" Putting the photo with Vinnie's, Noah returned the others to the folder and closed it.

"A few times, actually." Wade nodded. "We could never definitively prove it, but we knew Tony took care of Costa's wetwork."

"Wetwork?" Allie looked at them both.

It was Wade who answered. "Wetwork is a term used for killing people."

"Oh." Allie blinked. "So, this Tony was Costa's hit man?"

He nodded. "Apparently, he still is." Drawing in a cleansing breath, Wade added, "Ryan and I spent months trying to work the guy. We thought we might be able to turn him, but the chicken shit was more afraid of his boss than he was us. And since Costa was a master at making sure his dirty work couldn't fall back on him or his men, we never had enough hard evidence to pin him or any of Costa's men down." His eyes fell on Allie. "Until you."

"Okay." Noah stood and grabbed the two pictures. "Hunt's in a meeting across town, but as soon as he gets back, I'll pass this new information along and see where he wants to go from here."

With a nervous twinge to her sweet voice, Allie asked Noah, "You think your boss is going to make you turn me over to the Marshals?"

But before his partner could answer, Wade looked her square in the eyes and promised, "That's not happening."

"In the meantime, I guess you two can hang out here." Noah turned to Allie. "Maggie has an autopsy to perform, but I'm sure once she's done, she'd be happy to go get another coffee with you."

Allie opened her pretty mouth—probably to accept Noah's offer on his wife's behalf—but Wade cut in before that could happen.

"Actually, there's an errand I want to run."

"An errand?" His partner raised a brow.

"I want to swing by Jax's club. See if he's heard anything."

"Who's Jax?"

Meeting Allie's questioning gaze, he said, "Jax is a... friend. Sort of." Noah snorted, but Wade ignored it and continued. "He's a former Navy Seal-turned-P.I. Guy's a total smartass, but he's one of the best P.I.'s I've ever known."

"Jax is one of those guys you hate to like," Noah explained in his own terms. "He's arrogant and a pain in the ass, but Wade's right. Whether it be people or information, Jax will find it." Belatedly, he added, "One way or another."

Normally, it was the 'another' that worried Noah and Wade, alike. But this was Allie's life they were talking about.

Wade didn't care where the man's intel came from or how it was obtained...if there was a possibility Jax could help, Wade would overlook whatever sort of shit the man had to pull in order to give it.

8

"Wow." Allie looked around the empty dance club.

At some point—she wasn't sure exactly when—she'd started thinking of herself as Allie again, rather than Allison.

Probably has something to do with the mouthwatering man standing protectively to your right.

There was no 'probably' to it. In a few short days, and despite the craziness still surrounding them, Wade had somehow managed to make her feel more like her old self than she had in years. And last night... Oh, man, was last night something.

Wonderful. Magical. Incredible.

It was all those things, and more. She just prayed the authorities caught Costa soon so they could have a chance at something real.

"Pretty impressive, huh?" Wade's deep, rumbly voice broke through her thoughts.

"Huh?" It took a second for his question to resonate. "Oh, yes. It's great."

From the street, *Sin*—that was the club's name—looked

like any ordinary bar. But once you stepped inside, the place opened up into a huge space clearly designed for entertainment.

The walls and ceiling were painted black, and there was a long, elegant-looking bar to her right. Positioned along its front were red leather barstools, their tops in pristine condition and their metal pedestals looked shiny and new.

Behind the bar was an expansive mirror, the counter and shelves in front of it lined with every kind of liquor imaginable. Some she recognized, many she didn't. But she'd never been a big drinker, so that wasn't all that surprising.

In front of them was a large, tiled dance floor complete with a stage and professional-looking DJ system. And positioned on the two-story wall above that was a gigantic circular window.

Probably so this Jax guy could keep a close eye on things when the place was packed.

The place even smelled high-end. Not like the small dives she and her teacher friends used to go to every once in a blue moon. Those bars were nice enough, but the floors were always sticky and they smelled like cigarettes and booze.

Sin had a clean, almost fruity scent. It was pleasant and subtle, and not at all overpowering.

"It's so much bigger inside than it looks from the outside."

"That's because I designed it to be that way."

Allie and Wade both looked to the club's far right corner where a very large, *very* muscular man was walking in their direction. His hair was dark brown, or maybe even black, and the guy had to be at least six-four. His tight white t-shirt revealed a multitude of tattoos covering the man's neck, as well as what she could see of his chest and arms.

Holy smokes.

"Glad to see you're still upright, Crenshaw," the man spoke again. "Of course, you have me and that partner of yours to thank for that."

"Allie Andrews, meet Jax Monroe."

"It's nice to meet you, Mr. Monroe." Allie held out her hand.

"Mr. Monroe was my father." The guy's enormous hand swallowed hers. "Or as my half-brother and I like to call him, the sperm donor. You, sweet thing, can call me Jax."

Sweet thing? Allie and the beast of a man shook hands before she dropped hers back to her side.

"Where's your bodyguard?" Wade asked. "Expected him to stop us before we had a chance to come inside."

"Ivan?" Jax shook his head. "I gave him the night off. Guy's got a baby coming soon. Figured he needed to be home with his wife."

This man had a bodyguard? The guy looked like he could take out half an army by himself. With his bare hands.

"That was awfully nice of you."

"Yeah, well... I'm a nice guy."

Wade scoffed, but then his handsome face became serious. "You know, I never got the chance to thank you. I wouldn't be here if it wasn't for you."

To Allie, Jax smiled his famous I'm-the shit smile. "See?" He pointed to his own chest. "Nice guy."

"I have a favor."

"Figured you did. You guys never come around here unless you need something."

"You complaining?"

"Hell, no." Jax chuckled deep. "Feds aren't exactly good for business."

Allie was starting to see what Noah meant by Jax being a

guy he hated to like. He seemed to be the opposite of Wade and his partner in every single way... except she got the impression it was largely an act.

A show to make people *think* he was this big, tough bastard of a man. But in reality, she got the feeling that somewhere beneath all those muscles and tattoos lay the soul of a kind and, when he wanted to be, gentle man.

"Listen, I know I already owe you," Wade started again. "But this time, it isn't about me."

"Damn right, you owe me. And don't think I won't show up someday to collect." Jax sent her a smirk and a wink. Returning his focus to Wade, he asked, "What's up?"

"What do you know about Lorenzo Costa?"

"The mob boss who just escaped federal custody?" One of the man's gigantic shoulders shrugged. "Not a lot. Why?"

Wade looked at Allie and back to Jax. "I can trust you to keep what I'm about to tell you between us, yeah?"

"Seriously? I didn't build two highly successful businesses by gossiping like a fucking teenage girl. You got something to say, spit it out. Otherwise, I've got shit to do before I open for the night."

Allie could tell Wade was still hesitant to tell the man what he needed to hear. So she did it for him.

"I'm the one who testified against Costa five years ago," she blurted. Wade's head swung in her direction as Jax's eyes grew wide. "I saw him and another man murder my boss in cold blood," she continued. "And although they could never prove it, Costa had my parents killed as payback."

"Allie Andrews..." Jax let her name roll off his tongue. A second later, a flash of recognition ignited behind those same dark eyes. "You're Allison Andrews. I remember seeing you on the news when that story broke." He ran a hand over the dark, well-trimmed beard covering his strong jaw.

"Damn. That was some brave shit you did, going up against a man like that."

Brave or stupid. All these years later, and she still wasn't sure.

"After we got news of Allie's parents' deaths, Allie was placed in Witness Protection."

"WITSEC?" Jax looked at her again. "That had to be rough."

"Wasn't exactly the highlight of my life, no," she responded matter-of-factly.

For some reason, her words made Jax grin. "I like you." He turned to Wade. "I like her."

"So do I," Wade told the other man. "That's why I'm here."

"You need someone to guard you, Allie?" Jax looked back at her with an overly flirtatious grin. " 'Cause I'd be happy to oblige."

"She doesn't need you to fucking guard her," Wade growled. "And this isn't a goddamn joke."

"All right, all right." Jax raised his hands as a show of peace. To Allie, he said, "Sorry. Bad habit."

"It's okay." She smiled.

The guy was rough and crude, and clearly in need of a woman to calm his immature attitude. But for some reason, Allie couldn't help but like him.

Getting down to the nitty gritty, Wade said, "Somehow, Costa found out the Marshals had Allie hiding out in a little town in Texas. Two of his men showed up with guns. Tried to kill her. One of the assholes' bullets grazed her as she was running away, but thankfully, she managed to lose them and was able to get in touch with me."

Genuine concern fell over Jax's hardened expression. He began to visually search her body, his eyes stopping when they caught sight of the white bandage peeking out from beneath the sleeve of her t-shirt.

"Damn. You okay?"

"I'm fine," she assured him.

"Why'd you call Crenshaw for help?" Jax asked. Then he shook his head as if he remembered an important fact. To Wade, he said, "That's right. I almost forgot you transferred here from D.C."

"I was the lead on the case, and Allie was under my protection prior to the trial."

"Right, but don't people who go into WITSEC have handlers they can call if they're in trouble?"

"My handler was found dead yesterday." Allie willed herself not to tear up. "He'd been tortured to death."

Jax muttered a low curse. "Sorry to hear that."

"We're thinking that's how Costa knew where to send his men," Wade added to the conversation. "It's also why I don't feel comfortable letting the Marshals know where Allie is."

"Makes sense."

Wade got to the point of their visit. "Look, I need you to do some digging for me. See if you can figure out where Costa and the assholes working for him might be hiding out."

A look of understanding crossed Jax's chiseled face. "You think he's going to come after her again?"

"I'd bet my life on it." Wade nodded.

"Lorenzo Costa isn't a man who gives up," Allie chimed back in. "And he sure as hell isn't the kind of man who accepts defeat. He's not going to stop until I'm dead."

"Told you before, sweetheart." Wade reached for her hand. "That's not going to happen."

Allie's heart swelled with love for the well-meaning man. At the same time, she also felt a little sad. Because, no matter how many promises he made, he couldn't protect her twenty-four-seven.

And if there's one thing she'd learned about Costa, it was that if he wanted someone dead, he didn't let anyone get in his way.

"All right, man. I'll see what I can find out. Can't make any promises, though. Denver's a hell of a long way from Virginia."

"Well, seeing as how my old office in D.C. has zero leads, anything you come up with is better than what we've got now."

"I'll make some calls and let you know."

"Thanks, Jax." Wade held out his hands. "I appreciate it."

"Don't thank me yet. I may not be of much help." He shook Wade's hand. To Allie, Jax said, "It was very nice to meet you, Allie Andrews. And don't worry." He took her hand in his and raised it to his lips. Then, as if he were a knight and she his lady, he placed a gentle kiss on the back before releasing his gentle hold. "Your secret is safe with me.

Beside her, Wade rolled his eyes, and linked his fingers with hers. Turning for the door, he said, "Aaand that's our cue to leave."

"What?" Jax asked much-too-innocently. "Was it something I said?"

"Goodbye Jax!" Wade hollered back over his shoulder. "Call me if you find something."

"Yes, your highness!" Jax called out sarcastically from behind them.

Allie giggled as she and Wade stepped onto the sidewalk.

"What's so funny?" He stopped and glanced down at her.
"Uh...he is."

"Jax?" Wade made a face. "He's an arrogant asshole."

"An arrogant asshole who apparently helped save your life."

The truth was there in his storm cloud eyes.

"Fine. He's an arrogant asshole who occasionally does something nice for someone else."

Allie laughed again. "I bet he does nice things all the time. You just don't know it."

Turning them both so they were facing each other, Wade rested his hands on her hips and leaned in a bit closer. Dropping his voice to a low rasp, he asked, "Should I be jealous?"

"Of Jax?" She shook her head. "Of course not."

"You sure?"

Wade was absolutely adorable when he was jealous.

Raising onto her tiptoes, Allie planted a chaste kiss on Wade's lips and whispered, "I'm sure."

"Better be," he teased. "I'd hate to have to kick the arrogant ass's...well...ass."

They started laughing as they started for his car. Wade pressed his fob to unlock the doors and was reaching for the passenger side handle when the sound of tires squealing against pavement echoed through the early afternoon air.

Turning, they both searched for the source. Allie spotted the speeding car immediately.

Dark paint. Tinted windows. No license plate. And as it quickly approached them, the passenger window rolled down and she spotted a very large gun.

"Get down!" Wade yelled.

Everything seemed to happen all at once, yet to her, it seemed like a slow-motion movie.

A series of deafening pops rang out. Glass shattered behind her. Wade leaped through the air toward her, a look of alarm and fear marring his handsome face.

Allie hit the sidewalk with a hard thud, the back of her head smacking against the unforgiving concrete. With the weight of Wade's body protecting her, she could hear the muffled sound of the car speeding off, and then...

Nothing.

9

"Neither of you saw the shooter's face?"

"Sorry, Dec." Wade glared at his detective friend. "We were a little busy trying not to get our asses shot off."

Declan King was one of Denver's best and brightest major crimes detectives. He also happened to be one of Wade and Noah's good friends, as well as Jax's half-brother.

Though to look at them, you'd never know it.

Dec had the same dark hair as Jax, but his was shorter and the hair covering his jaw was more scruff than beard. And where Jax was damn near head-to-toe tattoos, Declan didn't have any. None that Wade had ever *seen*, anyway.

"He's just doing his job, Wade." Allie's small hand rested on Wade's lower back.

"Yeah, Crenshaw," Jax antagonized him. "Get off my brother's ass."

Though he knew the man was only goading him—because that's the sort of thing Jax did—the jackass was right. None of this was Dec's fault.

But Christ Almighty. Between knowing Costa's crew had

somehow figured out Allie was in Denver, and thinking she'd been hit…

Wade had never been more scared in his entire fucking life.

Before the gunfire had even ended, the former SEAL had come running out of *Sin*, his pistol raised and at the ready. Unfortunately, the shooters had already fled the scene.

"You should be in the hospital," he bit out more harshly than intended.

It had been nearly an hour since the shooting, the fear that he'd almost lost her right in front of him was still pulsing through his icy veins.

"The EMT's checked me over, remember?" She looked up at him. "I have a bump on my head, but I'm fine."

"You could be concussed."

It was a fucking miracle she hadn't been *killed*.

"I'm not."

"They didn't say you *weren't*," Wade reminded her. "They said they didn't suspect that you were, but they also suggested you go to the hospital for further testing to be sure."

And since he was busy giving his statement to Declan, he hadn't been there to stop her from signing the paper refusing treatment and sending the medics on their merry way.

Someone cleared their throat, and it took a full second for Wade to realize it was the man trying to grasp the full picture of what had happened.

"I'm sorry, Detective King." Allie all but dismissed his concerns. "You were saying?"

As if needing his permission, the man looked to Wade before continuing on with his questions. "Uh…I was asking if either of you got a look at the driver of the car or the shooter."

"No. I'm sorry." She started to shake her head but stopped herself with a poorly-hidden grimace. "Like Wade said, it all happened so quickly. Plus, the windows were heavily tinted."

"So you saw the gun, and then..."

"Wade knocked me to the ground." She looked up at him as if he were some sort of hero. *Not even close, sweetheart.* "Then he shielded me with his body until the gunfire stopped and the threat was gone."

"This was Lorenzo Costa." He'd bet his life on it.

Dec stared back at him. "You just said you didn't see their faces."

"Doesn't matter." Wade shook his head. "This was him."

"Well, given everything you've told me, you're probably right." Dec put his notebook and pen away. "But without proof, there's not a whole lot I can do."

"I gave your men access to my cameras outside," Jax spoke up again.

"You did, but they said the same thing. Tinted windows, no plates, and the shooter only rolled his window down far enough to fit the gun's barrel."

"So we got nothing." Wade clenched his jaw so tightly he was surprised his teeth didn't shatter. "*Fuck!*" He spun around and slammed his hand against the club's wooden bar.

The sharp sound seemed to fill the entire club.

"Listen, man. I know you're pissed, but sooner or later, guys like this...they always fuck up."

"Yeah?" He looked back at his friend. "Well it better be sooner, because the next time, we might not be so lucky."

Just then, Noah came rushing through Sin's splintered

door. His face was filled with concern. "Sorry, man. I got here as soon as I could." He gave Wade and Allie each an assessing glance. You two okay?"

"I am." Wade shot Allie a look. "She might have a concussion."

Allie sighed. "I have a bump and a couple bruises. Not a concussion."

Wade had texted Noah right after the shooting to let him know what happened, but his partner had been forty-five minutes away, chasing down an unexpected lead on another case.

"I've got Wright pulling traffic cam footage to see if we can figure out where the hell those guys went."

The guy really was the best partner ever.

"In the meantime, you two should consider staying someplace other than your apartment," Declan suggested. "If these guys know Miss Andrews is in town, they probably know it's because she's with you."

Shit. He hadn't even thought about that.

"I'd have you stay with me and Mags," Noah began. "But if they know you're guarding Allie, they've probably looked into you, too. Wouldn't be a stretch for them to think you might turn to me for safe keeping."

"I won't put you and Maggie in danger." Wade shook his head.

"That's a good point," Declan agreed. "You and Maggie might want to think about getting a hotel room for a few days. Just until things blow over."

The man didn't get it. This shit wasn't going to just *blow over*. None of this would be over until either Costa was in the ground...or Allie was.

And that last one wasn't a fucking option.

The image of her standing outside with bullets flying all

around her flashed through his mind. He could still see her lying there after, her eyes closed. Her body still.

I thought she was dead.

Unable to stand there a second longer, he turned to Declan. "You got everything you need?"

"Uh...yeah. I guess I do."

"Good." To Jax, he said, "I need a room for five minutes. Tops."

"Only five minutes?" Jax smirked. To Allie, he said, "Damn, honey. You have my sympathies."

"Jax," Wade hissed through his teeth. He was *not* in the mood for fucking jokes.

"Second door on your right down the hall." He motioned toward the club's back hallway. "Should be unlocked."

Without another word to anyone, Wade grabbed Allie's hand in a gentle-yet-stern hold and guided her across the club.

"Where are we going?" She asked.

He didn't answer.

Instead, Wade continued marching with purpose until they reached the door. He turned the knob, grateful as fuck that it was, as Jax said, unlocked.

Yanking open the door, he pulled her into the dark room and slammed the door shut behind her.

"Wade, what are you—"

He pushed her up against the door and slammed his mouth against hers. The fear he'd felt when they were under fire was still raging inside him like a feral beast. And if he didn't let it loose right the fuck now, Wade knew it would drive him insane.

Stunned, it took Allie a few seconds to catch up. But when she did, she grabbed hold of him tightly, her right leg wrapping around the back of his thighs and kissed him back as if he was her entire world.

She's my world. She's my everything.

Minutes later, after he'd finally, *finally* convinced himself she really was okay, Wade brought the savage kiss to an end. Pulling away slightly, he leaned his forehead against hers and panted his words as his chest heaved from his efforts to ease the terror coursing through him.

"I thought I lost you," he whispered. "I saw you lying there on the ground, and I thought..." He licked her taste from his lips. "I thought they'd taken you from me."

"But they didn't." Allie raised a hand and cupped one side of his face. Emotional tears welled in her eyes as she stared up at him. "I'm okay. I'm right here, and I'm okay. *We're* okay."

"I love you." Yeah, he just blurted that shit right out.

Funny, though. Wade didn't regret it one damn bit.

"W-what did you just say?" Allie was clearly shocked by his surprising declaration.

Lifting his head, Wade needed to look her in the eye when he said the words again. "I love you, Allie. And before you say anything, this isn't a, we-almost-died-so-I-feel-like-I-should-say-it sort of admission. I fell in love with you five years ago, and I *still* love you." He swallowed a knot of emotion that was threatening to choke him. "I know I've screwed things up before, but if you give me a chance, give *us* a chance, I swear I will do everything I possibly can to keep you safe...and make you happy."

He watched her face for any sign of disappointment or regret. But all he found in her baby blues were tears of what he prayed was happiness.

Wade held his breath and waited. Thankfully, she didn't make him wait long.

"I love you, too, Wade." Allie blinked, sending twin tears trickling down her flushed cheeks. "I've always loved you."

He released that breath with a whispered, "Thank God." Then he smiled as he leaned and pressed his lips to hers.

This kiss was different. It was one made of pure emotion, and the unspoken promise he'd lay his life on the line to keep her safe.

Allie held onto his shoulder and he framed her face with both hands. His tongue met hers, and as he held the most precious thing in his world close, they tasted one another like never before.

Seconds later, he regrettably pulled away once more. "I think our five minutes are up." He tucked some wayward strands behind her ear. "We should probably get back out there before Jax decides to do something stupid like barge in here."

"He'd do that?" Her brows arched high. "Even if he thought we were…"

"It's Jax, sweetheart. You never know what that crazy bastard's gonna do."

With a soft chuckle Allie pushed herself away from the door as he took a step back. Giving her a moment to compose herself, Wade snuck in one last kiss before opening the door and heading back out where the others were still waiting.

She'd ran her fingers through her hair, which helped, but there was nothing she could do to hide her red and swollen lips. Asshole that he was, Wade felt a sense of male pride knowing he was the reason for it.

Noah looked at him as if he were about to implode. "You good?"

Declan was gone, but Jax and Noah were still standing where they'd left them.

"I'm good." Wade nodded.

Maybe *good* was a bit of a stretch, but at least he no longer felt like his fear of losing her was going to eat him from the inside out.

Jax's knowing gaze bounced back and forth between Wade and Allie before he said, "So...back to where you two should stay. I know a place."

Wade blinked. "You do?"

"Yep." The big guy nodded.

"Where?"

"Here."

Wade laughed. "Okay."

"I'm serious." His expression said as much.

"You really expect us to stay here?" He glanced around. "I mean, no offense. You've got a kick-ass club, but it's going to be filled with people every single night. Doesn't exactly scream safe house."

"That's my whole point." When Wade opened his mouth to say thanks, but no thanks, Jax cut him off at the pass. "Look, just hear me out. I did remodeling upstairs. My office is still there, but now there's also a one-bedroom studio apartment. It's small but has all the essentials. King sized bed, kitchen, bathroom...it even has a shower. Plus, it just got finished a few days ago, so I haven't even used it yet.

"That sounds great, except for the whole dance-club part. I've seen the crowds this place draws in, Jax. It would be a security nightmare."

"I disagree."

"What do you mean?" Noah spoke up.

"I can post a guard in the front and back. I've got enough guys I trust, they can take shifts so the place is covered twenty-four-seven."

Wade considered this, but it still wasn't enough. "The

people after Allie just shot your place all to hell. This is the *last* place she should be."

"I'll have the front fixed by lunch time tomorrow. As for the other, that's the perfect reason for you two to stay here."

"Why do you say that?" Allie spoke up.

"Because, darlin'. These guys aren't going to expect you to be holed up in a nightclub. Especially one they just hit. And the guys who work for me?" Jax continued his efforts to convince him. "They're not a bunch of rent-a-cops I found working mall security. These guys are all fully vetted, former military men who are well-trained and loyal as fuck. I tell them to do it, they do it."

"Hate to say it, partner," Noah took Jax's side. "But the man does have a point."

Glancing down at Allie, Wade considered his options. Which weren't many.

They could go to a hotel, but that still left them somewhat vulnerable. Plus, knowing Costa, the bastard would probably end up sending his goons to check out every single one in the city.

He could get Hunt to set him up at a safe house somewhere out of town, but then his resources were limited. If something did go down, backup would be too far out to be of any use.

And then there was the third option. Staying here.

Well, shit.

"Fine. But so help me, anything happens to her while we're here, I swear to Christ—"

"You'll kill me." Jax blew the threat off. "Yeah, I get it."

To Allie, Wade asked, "You okay with this?"

"Do we really have another option?"

No. Unfortunately, they didn't.

"We could have a couple cars parked along the block, too. I'm sure Hunt would approve it," Noah offered.

"Yes." Jax rolled his eyes. "Because nothing says inconspicuous like a bunch of Feds parked outside the damn place."

And the arrogant asshole has returned.

"We'll need to get some things from my place. Clothes, toiletries..."

"Make a list." Noah nodded. "I'll take care of it."

"There's a notepad and pen behind the bar," Jax offered.

Walking around the counter's edge, Wade spotted the small lined notepad right away. After jotting down a few things for himself, he handed it across the bar to Allie for her to add whatever she wanted Noah to grab. With the list in hand, Noah said a quick goodbye with a promise to return ASAP.

Once he was gone, Jax turned to them and smiled. "Let's go see your temporary home, shall we?"

With her hand in his, Wade and Allie followed the P.I. slash club owner up to the second floor. As they walked, he stole a few glances at the woman beside him and thought about what Jax had just dubbed his new apartment.

Temporary home.

That had been Allie's entire life for the last several years. First in Salado, then his apartment. Now this one...

His heart ached for all she'd been through, but he made a silent vow to do whatever he had to do to give her everything she wanted...for the rest of their lives.

I'll get you a forever home soon, sweetheart. I swear I will.

10

"We'll get them, Wade." Allie walked over to where he stood at the small kitchen sink. With her hand caressing his back, she reiterated the statement with, "We *will*."

Turning around, he leaned his butt against the edge of the counter and pulled her into his arms. "I know." He hugged her close. "I just hate that you're going through all of this again."

"It's not just me, you know." She looked up at him. "You forget, you could've been killed today, too."

She couldn't stop seeing it. The car. The gun. The shattered glass and panic on Wade's face.

No, that was wrong. He hadn't panicked. He'd reacted like the trained agent he was. And like the man who loved her, he'd risked himself in order to keep her safe.

He loves me.

Allie still couldn't believe those precious words had fallen from his kissable lips. Despite the madness surrounding them, and the threats that were still out there, that moment will forever be engrained in her memories as her favorite.

The only things that could top it would have to happen later. After they were done hiding out in a stranger's upstairs apartment over a nightclub.

Jax had closed the place down for the night since the window and door were still all boarded up. It was a shame, because Allie rather thought it might be fun to forget their troubles and go downstairs and dance.

Of course, Wade would never go for that. Especially tonight. Not that she could blame him.

On to plan B.

"You want to watch a movie?" she asked, having the sudden urge to act like a normal couple. Even if it was just for a few hours.

"Sure." He gave her a small smile. "There was some popcorn in the groceries Jax had delivered. I could pop a bag if you want?"

"That sounds great."

"Okay, then. You go pick a movie, and I'll be in as soon as it's done."

With a quick peck on her cheek, Wade went in search of the popcorn while she headed for the couch. She wasn't really hungry, but her desire to forget all their troubles for one night was fierce.

After Jax brought them upstairs and gave them the nickel tour, he surprised them both by having a couple pizzas delivered for dinner, plus enough groceries to get them by for several days.

They'd just finished eating the pizza when Noah and Maggie arrived with their things from Wade's apartment. After a short conversation, they left to go stay...someplace. Allie wasn't quite sure where the kind man was taking his wife.

God, she hated this. Everyone she'd grown to care about

had either already been hurt—or in her parents' case, killed—or they were now having to uproot their lives in order to stay safe. All because of her.

Damn it, Allison. This. Is. Not. Your. Fault!

The voice in her head was right, and it was high time she started putting the blame where it belonged. Costa was a monster, and until he was either caught or dead, no one was going to be safe.

You're supposed to be pretending to be normal, remember?

Normal. Right. Okay.

Allie picked up the remote as the sound of kernels popping filled the small space. Rolling through the countless movie channels Jax's satellite subscription included, she couldn't believe it when she came to Wade's favorite.

And it was just about to start.

"You find something to watch?" He carried in a big plastic bowl filled to the brim.

"Sure did." Allie smirked. She pressed play and waited for his reaction.

The second the intro started, his eyes widened as they flew to hers. "No way!"

"How's that for some good luck?"

He sat the bowl down onto the small coffee table in front of them. "About damn time we had some of that."

Leaning over, he planted a chaste kiss on her lips and whispered, "I love you."

Man, she would never get sick of hearing that. "I love you, too."

He kissed her again. And again.

They *kept* kissing, and the next thing Allie knew, the movie was over, and their clothes were in a scattered pile on the floor.

Half-on and half-under him, Allie snuggled in closer as she lay next to him. Satiated and feeling perfectly normal.

"Think Jax will be mad we christened his new couch before he could?"

Wade considered this for a moment before he said, "I don't care."

Laughing, she pushed herself up and picked up the remote to turn off the T.V. Grabbing her clothes from the floor, she said, "I think I'll shower before heading to bed. Care to join me?"

The apartment was small, but the shower was the largest she'd ever seen. Of course, given Jax's enormous frame, it came as no surprise.

"As a matter of fact..."

Unabashedly, Wade stood and held out his hand. His swallowed hers up as she placed her hand in his and allowed him to help her to her feet.

Allie followed him across the small apartment and into the bathroom. It took a few seconds for the water to heat up, but then the two of them stepped into the custom-made area and stood beneath the giant overhead showerhead.

"This is heaven." She closed her eyes and let the water rain down on her.

"Yes." Wade's hands gripped her hips as he pulled her body flush with his. "It is."

Lifting her lids, Allie found him staring down at her as if she were the most important thing in his world. She shook her head, still in awe of what had transpired between them.

Her mom had once told her true love often came when a person least expected it. Turned out, she was right.

"When this is all over, we should go away somewhere. Not because we're hiding, or bad people are after us...just to relax and enjoy each other's company."

He grinned. "You have someplace in mind?"

"I don't know..." Allie thought for a moment. "Maybe a beach somewhere?"

She could have driven to the beach a hundred times when she lived Salado, but for some reason the idea of going by herself wasn't all that appealing. But going there with Wade?

I'd go anywhere with him.

"A beach would be nice." Wade reached up and gently began kneading her breasts. His thumbs moved upward, their callused pads rubbing her distended nubs. "You know what sounds even better?"

Despite her recent thoughts of being completely satisfied, Allie's sex became full and needy once again. Apparently, Wade was experiencing the same rush of arousal because his cock filled and was pressing against her lower belly.

"What would be better than a beach?" She arched into his touch.

He leaned down, his lips running along the length of her jaw. His scruff tickled her skin as he left tiny kisses down the side of her neck.

Closing her eyes, Allie tilted her head to give him better access. At the same time, she slid a hand between them and began stroking his wet shaft at a slow and steady pace.

Wade hissed in a breath and said, "A wedding on the beach."

Her hand stopped. Her entire freaking *world* stopped.

Allie's eyes flew open, and she looked up at the crazy man. "A *wedding*? Are you nuts?"

Surely, he wasn't serious. He couldn't be. They'd only reconnected a few days ago, and just today shared their true feelings for one another.

"I *am* nuts." He brushed the tip of his nose to hers. "I'm nuts about you."

"But Wade, we—"

"Do you love me?"

His question stopped her short. "Of course, I love you."

"And I love *you*. So why wait, when we both know where this is headed."

She stared up at him feeling a little off-balance by what he was saying. "Where is this headed?"

"Marriage. Kids." He ran a fingertip down the side of her damp cheek. "We can even get a dog, if you'd like."

"A dog?" Allie smirked.

"Or a cat. But if we go that route, I have to warn you. I don't do litter boxes."

She chuckled, but stopped when his expression became as serious as she'd ever seen it. "I want it all with you, sweetheart. I know were in the middle of a shitstorm, but it'll pass. And when it does, I want you to be my wife."

Well, when he put it like that…

"Okay." Allie smiled up at him.

"Okay? As in…you'll marry me?"

She figured she must be nuts, too, because the only answer that felt right was, "Yes, I'll marry you."

Wade's face lit up with the biggest, widest smile as he lifted her up and brought his mouth to hers.

With water still pouring down over them, Allie let out a tiny squeal, then laughed. "You know this is insane, right?"

"I don't care." He kissed her again. "I just want you to be mine."

Didn't he already know? "I am yours, Wade." She brushed her lips against his. "I always have been."

Her words—and the fact that they were freaking *engaged*—must have spurred something inside him, because the next thing Allie knew, her back was up against the shower wall and Wade's hand was between her legs.

She gasped as he ran a finger down the length of her slit. They'd had sex less than an hour ago, yet her body was aching desperately. Her core drenched with arousal.

Never enough.

The realization struck as he pushed one of his fingers inside. Allie knew to the depths of her soul that when it came to this man, it would never be enough.

"You're so wet," his deep voice sounded of sex and passion. He thrust his finger in and out at a slow, torturous rate.

"Wade," Allie whispered his name as she wrapped her right leg around his hip and pulled him closer.

She needed more. She needed *him*.

As if reading her mind, Wade added a second digit. His hand moved faster. Harder.

Allie closed her eyes and laid her head back against the warm ceramic tile. Steam billowed around them as she became consumed by the pleasure only he could give.

Her hips jolted when she felt his fingers on her swollen clit. Allie dug her fingernails into his shoulders and held on as he brought her to the edge of that beautiful cliff.

"Wade," she panted his name a second time. Almost as if she were begging him. Maybe she was.

"That's it, baby." He moved his fingers in a tight, circular motion. "Come on. There you go."

Between his words and the glorious way he played her body like a finely tuned instrument, Allie felt herself climbing higher and higher.

Her breaths heaved, and her legs began to tremble. Her lower belly tingled, a sign that she was almost there.

Wade pressed harder, but not too hard. He held onto her

hip with his other hand, his raging erection pressing against her inner thigh as he brought her to the brink.

Almost there. Just a little more.

Just. Like. *That!*

Allie cried out as the orgasm hit. Her entire body felt weightless, as if she were flying.

"Fucking beautiful," Wade growled. He continued working her body until the pressure became too much to bear.

Sensing this, he pulled his hand away, keeping her steady as she lowered her leg and attempted to remain upright.

"Wow." Allie looked back at him through a pair of heavily-lidded eyes.

"Tell me about it." He grinned, nibbling her bottom lip.

They stood like that for what seemed like forever as she regained control of her limp and sated body. When her mind cleared and her strength returned, Allie decided it was time to take care of him.

She dropped to her knees, uncaring of the slight bight from the shower's tiled floor.

"Sweetheart, you don't have to—"

Wade started to pull her back up, but Allie stopped him. "I know I don't have to." She stared up at him. "I want to."

Without giving him a chance to protest further, she took him in her hand and wrapped her lips around his swollen tip. Wade's entire body jerked from the intimate contact, but she didn't dare stop.

Instead, Allie sucked him in slowly. Inch by inch, she filled her mouth with his hot, solid shaft. He tasted warm and slightly salty, his body already weeping with desire.

She moved up and down slowly, running her tongue along the swollen crown as she did. Wade's hand gripped the back of her head, his fist filling with her wet hair as she continued making love to him with only her mouth.

His hips moved forward, keeping pace with the steady rhythm she'd set. Through the sound of running water, Allie could hear his heady breaths and deep, rumbling moans.

She smiled around him, loving that she could bring him as much pleasure as he had her. Teasing with her tongue again, she felt the slight sting in her scalp when his grip tightened in response.

Allie began to move faster. She sucked harder. Adding her fist, she worked him up and down in almost a frantic race to the finish.

Wade became impossibly harder as his breathing grew more erratic. Knowing he was close encouraged her to do whatever it took to make him feel what she'd felt.

"Jesus, Allie," he panted. "I'm close. Really...fucking...close."

Yeah, she gathered that.

With no intentions of stopping, Allie added a little twist to her wrist as she pumped him in and out of her mouth. He was almost there. She could *feel* it. But just when she started to hollow her mouth in preparation for what she knew was inevitable, he pulled himself free.

"What are you..."

"Inside you." Wade lifted her to her feet. "Now."

Spinning her around, Allie slapped the palms of her hands against the shower wall. Wade grabbed her hips and pulled her lower half toward him so her ass was in the position he needed.

"Spread your legs," he ordered.

She did as she was asked.

Wade's warmth enveloped her as he brought their bodies together. He bent at his knees, positioning his hot tip to her already-drenched entrance. Then, without waiting, he entered her in one, long thrust.

"Ah!" She threw her head back.

"You okay?" His lips brushed against her ear.

Was he kidding? 'Okay' didn't even *begin* to describe what she was.

"Yeah," Allie somehow managed to choke out.

Taking her at her word, Wade wasted no time. He began to move, his hips smacking against her bare ass with each thrust.

The sound of wet flesh slapping together echoed off the tiled walls. It was erotic as hell, and Allie suddenly found herself pushing back against him in an effort to bring him as much pleasure as she possibly could.

"Not...gonna...last..." Wade spoke between thrusts.

His glorious cock slid in and out of her needy core. Unbelievably, Allie found herself on the brink of yet *another* orgasm. Something she wouldn't have thought possible.

Knowing Wade was occupied with his own impending release, she decided to help herself get there faster.

Reaching down, she kept one hand on the wall, using the other to work her clit with familiar ease. Like a piston, he pushed himself in and out harder while her hand moved frantically between her thighs.

"Jesus, that's hot," Wade rasped. "That's it, baby. Make yourself come."

As if her body had been waiting for his permission, Allie was hit with her third climax of the night. This one wasn't as strong as the others, yet it still filled her vision with bright, shiny stars.

Wade's body jerked behind her. His thrusts becoming erratic.

He pushed inside her once. Twice. And on the third, he found his release.

"Allie!" He came inside her, her name releasing from his lips with an animalistic growl.

Soon, his movements slowed as he drew out the remnants of what felt like a powerful climax. And when he pulled himself out, Wade wrapped his arms completely around her so he could hold her close.

"I think you almost killed me." His voice was rough and gravely.

Allie chuckled lazily and turned around to face him. "I could say the same about you."

Resting his forehead against hers—a move she was quickly learning she loved—Wade held her like that until their racing hearts returned to normal and the water's heat began to cool.

Later, as Allie lay in the warmth and safety of his arms, she knew with utter certainty that she'd found her missing half. Now all that was left was to get free of the threats hanging over her.

Because until that happened, all thoughts of love, marriage, and happy-ever-after were just another dream.

11

Two days later...

"What the hell do you mean, he's presumed dead?" Wade's stomach dropped as he gripped the phone tightly.

Noah's search through the traffic cams had ended when the car involved in the drive-by disappeared down a side street with no cameras. Jax had several feelers out, but they hadn't gotten back with him yet, and since Wade still hadn't heard from his old partner, and the messages he'd left had gone unanswered, he'd weighed the risks and decided to call his old boss back in D.C.

The answer he'd been given came as a huge fucking shock.

"I'm sorry. I know you two were tight back in the day." SAC Brian Reynolds offered his condolences. "We're all still reeling from the news, ourselves."

Ryan was dead? He couldn't believe it.

"What the fuck happened?"

There was a pause and then, "We're not releasing the

details just yet, so this needs to stay out of the public eye." After Wade's quick assurance, Reynolds said, "Landry didn't show up for work a couple days ago. At first, we thought maybe he was home with the same stomach bug that's been going around here and forgot to call in. I left a message for him to call me back, but after a few hours went by without a word, I sent a couple agents to his place to check on him."

"And?"

"And his place had been trashed. There were obvious signs of a struggle, and...." His former boss paused, clearly fighting through his emotions. "Ryan's body wasn't there, but there was blood everywhere."

Sonofabitch.

Wade closed his eyes, willing his mind not to picture Ryan going through the same fate as John Napier. "And you're *sure* it was his?"

It was a desperate question, but one Wade had to ask.

"Lab confirmed the match," Reynolds told him what he already knew. "I went to his house, Wade. There were two bullets in his living room wall. One matched Landry's service weapon. The other came back to a weapon used in one of our old cases. I'm sure you can guess the main suspect in that one."

"Costa," Wade practically spit the man's name out as if it were a curse.

"Got it in one."

"Okay, so there's evidence of a shooting, but what makes you think Ryan's dead?" The guy could've been taken somewhere to be tortured, for all they knew.

"In addition to the pool of blood we found at his place, a witness also saw two men dumping a car into Kingman Lake just off of Benning Road. She immediately called it in, and a dive crew was sent out. They pulled the car to the surface, Wade. It was Landry's."

The sliver of hope Wade had been feeling at the beginning of the call was dwindling away at an alarming rate.

"They found his car, but not his body?"

It was funny how, despite hearing the damning facts, he still couldn't seem to let go of the possibility that his friend was still alive.

"Divers said trunk had popped open when the car hit the bottom of the lake. We'd had heavy rains here in the days prior, so the water level was high, and the current was stronger than normal. They think his body was washed down river into the Potomac. And you know as well as I do how low the chances are of finding a body once it hits those waters."

Yeah. Unfortunately, he did.

"There's more."

Those two words raised Wade's sense of dread to the next level. "Tell me."

"You remember the A.D.A. who worked Costa's trial?"

"Kyle Young?" Wade nodded. "Yeah, I remember him." The guy could be a pain in the ass, but he was a damn good trial lawyer.

"He was found in the courthouse parking garage. Bastards shot him in the head while he was still in his car."

Jesus Christ. Wade fell back onto Jax's couch and ran a frustrated hand down his face. These guys weren't just after Allie. They were taking out everyone involved in the case.

"They're targeting the key players involved in Costa's trial," Reynolds parroted his thoughts. "The judge has been put into protective custody, so for now, he's safe. But you and Miss Andrews need to watch your backs."

That last part had him sitting straight up. "Miss Andrews?" Wade asked carefully.

"Come on, Crenshaw. This is me you're talking to, remember? You think I didn't see the bond you two formed back in the day? The second news broke of Costa's escape, I knew you'd do whatever it took to get to her. Especially when the Marshals called here asking if we knew where she'd run off to."

Well, fuck. He'd always known the man was sharp, but damn. "We're staying safe."

The man's smug smirk practically oozed through the phone. "Glad to hear it. And don't worry...as far as I'm concerned, you and I haven't spoken since you left this office five years ago."

Always did like you, Reynolds.

"Thanks." Wade offered the man his sincere appreciation. Filling his lungs with a cleansing breath, he asked, "You got any leads?"

"No, but Lorenzo Costa didn't get away with the shit he pulled all those years by being stupid. The man knows how to lay low. He also knows how to leave a crime scene so it can't be connected to him."

Wasn't that the fucking truth. "All right. Do me a favor? If something does come up—"

"You'll be the first one I call."

"Thanks, Brian.

"Of course. Oh, and Crenshaw?" The other man caught him just before he ended the call.

"Yeah?"

"Try not to get your ass killed."

Despite the situation, Wade smiled. "Roger that."

The other line went dead, a signal that his former boss had hung up.

Tapping the first number in his contact list, Wade was just about to call Noah and fill him in when Allie stepped out of the bathroom.

"Was that Noah?"

Wade shook his head. "My former boss back in D.C."

"Oh." She blinked, surprised. "Did he have news on Costa?"

In a manner of speaking. "Come here." He patted the cushion next to him.

Wariness filled her pretty eyes. "Uh oh. This can't be good."

No. No, it wasn't.

Waiting for her to sit, Wade linked his fingers with hers and gave her the news. By the time he was done, Allie's skin had paled, and the sympathy she felt for his old partner was clear.

"Oh, my God." She stared down at their joined hands. "I always liked Agent Landry. He was really nice to me."

"Yeah." Wade's voice broke as he thought of his friend. "Ryan is a…" He swallowed hard. "Ryan *was* a good man."

A good man. Good agent. And an even better friend.

"I'm so sorry, Wade." Allie laid her head on his shoulder.

She didn't say anything more, but she didn't need to. Just having her here, by his side, was all the comfort he needed.

With a short sniff, Wade blinked away the tears threatening to form and cleared his throat. Once he'd regained his composure, he picked up his phone and called Noah. He put it on speaker so Allie could hear, too.

"Hey, man." Noah greeted him. "I was just about to head that way."

"You have news?"

"No, but I wanted to see how you two were holding up. Figured you might need a friendly face after being locked away with Jax as your only source to the outside for the last two days."

Wade smiled. "Believe it or not, but the guy's actually been pretty decent to deal with."

"That's because the more he does for us, the more we owe him."

A factual statement, but as long as he was helping to keep Allie safe, Wade would be content owing the guy for the rest of his life.

"If you don't need anything, then I think I'll keep working. Wright's working his computer magic trying to find some sort of financial tie to either Costa or one of his crew."

"He really think that's out there?" Wade had little faith that these guys were that stupid.

"Don't know, but it's not like we have much else to go on right now." Noah's exhale filled the phone's speakers. "These guys have to be staying somewhere, and now that we know *they* know Allie's here in Denver, they're not going to go far."

Not until they've completed the job they were hired to do, anyway.

"I assume you're looking into his crew's backgrounds?" That's where Wade would start.

"Wright's running every report he can think of to find some sort of local tie to one of them. These guys are good, but we're better. We're looking at properties, former classmates, cell mates, relatives...everything and anything to figure out where they're holed up."

Good. That was good.

"We'll find them, Wade. We're not going to stop until we do."

"Thanks." Wade released a slow breath. "Listen, I talked to my old boss back in D.C."

A few seconds of silence passed before Noah said, "Yeah? You find out anything useful?"

He told Noah everything he'd learned. Ryan's presumed murder, the A.D.A., all of it.

"Shit, man. I'm sorry."

"Thanks."

There was another pause and then, "You know what this means, right?"

"That they're gunning for me, too?" Wade met Allie's anxious stare. "Yeah. I know."

"Never thought I'd say this, but I'm glad you're staying at Jax's place. He may be an asshole, but he's a loyal one. And those guys he has working for him are the real deal."

"You checked them out?"

"Hell yes, I had them checked out. You're my partner, Wade," Noah reminded him. "You really think I'm going to trust complete strangers to have your back…and Allie's… without knowing if they can be trusted?"

"Aww, stop it," he teased. "You're gonna make me blush."

"Smartass."

"Better than being a dumbass."

Noah chuckled. "Glad to see this whole thing hasn't stolen your sense of humor."

"Nah." Wade gave Allie's hand a squeeze. "It's going to take a whole lot more than some dipshit mobster to do that."

Especially when the other part of his life—the best part—was starting to work out exactly as he'd always wanted.

He didn't get into the whole impromptu-engagement discussion. Mostly because Wade wanted to keep that just between him and Allie. For now.

"All right, man." Noah brought the conversation to a close. "I'm going to go up and see if Wright's made any headway. I'll call you later, hopefully with something useful."

"Thanks. Catch you later."

Ending the call, Wade put his arm around Allie and pulled her close. He kissed the top of her head and leaned his cheek against her hair.

"Noah's a good friend," she said softly.

"Yeah." Wade agreed. "He is."

Hours later, Allie was standing at the stove, cooking something that smelled amazing when Wade walked in to join her.

Walking up behind her, he wrapped his arms around her waist and dropped a soft kiss onto her neck, just below her ear. "Anything I can do to help?"

"You can taste this and tell me how it is."

Lifting a wooden spoon to his lips, she gave him a tiny sample of the sauce she was making to go with the chicken sautéing in a pan to her right.

Wade sucked the savory concoction between his lips, and the let explosion of flavor hit the tip of his tongue. "Wow." His brows shot up. "That's amazing. What is it?"

"A garlic lemon sauce with sautéed shallots, sea salt, and a white wine reduction."

"I don't know half of what you just said, but it's delicious."

A prideful smile graced her beautiful face. "Thanks. It's one of my favorite recipes."

Stepping to the side, he leaned his ass against the counter and watched her do her thing. "Where did you learn to cook like that?"

"Food shows and Pinterest, mainly." She moved the

saucepan to one of the back burners and turned off the heat to the one she'd been using. "When I first moved to Salado, I didn't know anyone, and it took a bit to find a job. I stayed inside as much as possible those first few months because I was so paranoid about being recognized. I got bored, so I started trying out new recipes."

"I'm sorry you were so alone." He ran the back of his knuckles down the length of her arm.

"Not your fault." She turned the chicken breasts over to brown the other side. "I know that, now."

Wade turned to face her more directly. "You know, we haven't talked a lot about the whole engagement thing."

"What's there to talk about? You asked, I accepted."

"Well, right." He chuckled. "But I was just wondering what your thoughts were about after."

"After?" Allie pulled down two plates from the cabinet directly above her.

"Yeah. You know, like…where we're going to live."

Still focused on the task at hand, she shrugged casually. "I assumed we'd live at your apartment."

"And we can, but I was thinking we could build a place. Maybe a house with a view of the mountains."

She stopped and looked at him. "Are you serious?"

"Why not? I've got a good chunk of money saved up, and it would be a hell of a lot better than my dingy, one-bedroom bachelor pad." A thought slapped him square in the jaw. "Unless you don't want to live in Denver."

"I'd *love* to live here. I mean, I haven't had much time to see the city, obviously, but I've always loved the idea of living near the mountains. Besides that, I'd never ask you to uproot your job and life for me."

Didn't she know? He'd move halfway around the world, if that's what it took to make her happy.

"This isn't all about me, Al. You have just as much of a say in our future as I do."

"I appreciate that." She leaned up and kissed him softly. "But I'm good here. You have your job, and I already have a friend in Maggie...and there are plenty of schools for me to teach in, once I get my Colorado certification."

So she's been thinking about all of this stuff, too. Good to know.

"And the idea of having a home of my own...I haven't had that in, well, ever. I lived with my parents until I went to college, then I had my townhouse, but that was a rental, so it doesn't count. After that was the tiny apartment in Salado, and then I came here. Plus, I could...no, we could design it and decorate it any way we wanted. How fun would that be?"

Seeing how big her smile was at just the *thought* of building a place of their own? Oh, yeah. That was all the fun he'd ever need.

Allie took the chicken out of the pan and placed one breast on each of the two plates. Turning off the stove, he watched as she used the same wooden spoon to scoop up the mouthwatering sauce and drizzle a generous amount over the chicken.

"There's a salad in the fridge, if you want to grab it," she told him.

Happy to oblige, Wade had just opened the refrigerator door when something caught his attention from the corner of his eye. Turning, his heart kicked against his ribs when he realized what it was.

Smoke.

"What the fuck?"

"What's wrong?" Allie looked at him from over her shoulder.

"Sweetheart, I don't want you to panic, but there's smoke coming in from under the door."

"*What?*"

Their chicken dinner forgotten, they both rushed over to the apartment's door. Careful not to burn himself, Wade tapped his fingertips to the metal knob to see if it was hot.

It was.

Sonofabitch!

"Call nine-one-one," he ordered.

While Allie ran to her phone to dial the three emergency digits, Wade grabbed the throw blanket from the back of the couch and used it to protect his hand. Turning the knob slowly, he cracked open the door.

A plume of gray smoke rolled into the apartment, and it only took him half a second to realize the entire hallway was filled.

Why the hell didn't the smoke detectors go off? And where the fuck is Jax and his men?

Wade looked around for another way out but remembered there was only one window in the small space, and it didn't have a fire escape below it. Somewhere the back of his mind, it registered that it could be a trap to lure them outside, but if they didn't get out now, they were both going to die.

"The fire department is on their way." Allie coughed. "They said because of the construction, it would take about ten minutes for them to get here.

They didn't have ten minutes. The apartment was already starting to fill with smoke.

Wade ran to the small stand by the bed and grabbed his phone, wallet, and gun. Rushing back into the kitchen, he yanked out two dish towels from one of the smaller drawers. Soaking them with cold water, he tossed one to Allie.

"Use that to cover your nose and mouth."

Clearly scared, she followed his directions without question.

The last thing Wade did was pull the comforter off the bed to have something to help protect Allie as they exited the building. That was assuming they could even *get* out.

Coughing, he told her, "When I open this door again, there's going to be a lot of smoke. Keep the damp cloth over your mouth and nose until we get outside."

"Okay," her voice was muffled.

"Not trying to be an asshole, here, but if I tell you to do something—"another cough—"I need you to do it without arguing. No matter what it is."

"Okay," she repeated.

By now, they were both having trouble talking without breaking out into a coughing fit. They needed to move their asses. Now.

Please let her get out safely.

With that quick silent pray sent to the heavens, Wade covered her with the comforter and opened the door. The smoke was thick and blinding, making his eyes burn on contact.

Knowing the building's layout, he helped her keep her head down as they turned left down the hallway and began inching their way toward the stairs he couldn't see.

Jesus, the smoke was damn near overpowering. But the sheer will to live and determination to get the woman he loved to safety pushed him on.

Allie began coughing so hard, her entire body shook beneath the blanket. Wade knew her lungs were on fire, because his felt the same damn way.

I'll get you out of here, sweetheart. You're going to be okay.

When they finally made it to the top of the stairs, Wade

caught his first glimpse of flames. Their flickering light served as a macabre guide to where they needed to go, but as they carefully made their way closer to the bottom, he realized the club's entire first floor was completely engulfed.

Including the last two steps it would take for them to get there.

"Wade?" Allie's strained voice reached his ears over the roar of the flames.

"It's okay, sweetheart. We're going to make it."

As he continued guiding her down the smokey staircase, Wade prayed it wasn't a lie. When they got to the third to the last step, he knew he didn't have a choice.

"We have to jump," he yelled, followed by a round of coughing. Damn, he never realized how *loud* a raging fire could be. "I'll go first and catch you!"

Allie didn't hesitate. "Okay."

Fuck, his eyes felt like they were filled with red-hot sand, but he didn't dare waist a single second trying to fix something that was unfixable.

Using the wall-mounted rail to his right for leverage, Wade leaped over the stairs and through the flames, landing in a spot clear of flames. With fire whipping all around him, he ignored the heat licking at his legs and held out his arms.

"Jump!" he yelled.

With trust reflected in her red and watery eyes, Allie tossed the comforter behind her. Following his lead, she grabbed the railing, reared herself back, and jumped.

She didn't make it quite as far as he had, but Wade was there, ready to pull her from the flames, if needed. Thankfully, between her momentum and his strength, she cleared the bottom step with inches to spare.

With her hand in his, they both coughed and hacked their way through the club toward the front door. Weaving over and around the small spots of flooring that were on fire, they rushed to the entrance, but when they got there, the door leading to the outside refused to open.

"It's jammed!" he pointed out the obvious.

Swinging around to the small tables on his right, Wade grabbed the first chair he could and lifted it above his head. Praying he wasn't about to cause some sort of backdraft, he heaved the chair toward the window Jax had only just replaced and turned away to shield his face from any flying shards that may come back his way.

Wade picked up a second chair, using it to clear out an opening safe enough for Allie to go through without the risk of getting cut. Pulling his gun from his back waistband, he kept it at the ready while using his free hand to carefully guide her through the makeshift hole and out onto the sidewalk.

They made it out just as the sound of sirens started blaring in the distance.

"Oh, my God!" Allie coughed some more as she turned to assess the damage. "I can't believe that just happened. I wonder what caused it."

"Not what." Wade hacked up some thick mucus and spit it out to the side. "Who."

"What?" Allie turned and followed his gaze.

Lying lifeless on the ground in front of the door was one of the men Jax had hired to stand guard. He'd been shot once, right in the heart.

Allie covered her mouth with her hand, her terrified eyes flying up to his. "But h-how did they know we were here?"

"I don't know." Wade shook his head. "But I'm damn sure going to find out."

12

ALLIE REMOVED the paper-thin hospital gown and pulled the clean t-shirt up over her head. Maggie had stopped by a few moments before, and the sweet M.E. had bought her a clean shirt, jeans, socks, and even *shoes* so Allie wouldn't have to put her smoke-ruined clothes back on once she was ready to leave.

Her hair and skin still reeked from the fire, but there wasn't anything that could be done about that until she was able to take a shower. Allie blinked several times, resisting the urge to rub her red, itchy eyes. The nurse had given her drops, but said there wasn't a lot they could do, and she'd just have to wait for the irritation to fade.

Upon Wade's insistence, she'd been properly checked out by an emergency room doctor this time. And after their harrowing escape and the discovery of that poor man's body, she'd been too mentally and physically exhausted to argue.

So after several pokes and prods, X-Rays to make sure her lungs were clear and not building up fluid, and having to lay in bed for what felt like forever to have her oxygen levels monitored, she'd *finally* been given a clean bill of health and was told she could leave.

It had been several hours since Jax's beautiful nightclub had burned to the ground. From what Maggie had told her, the firefighters had done what they could, but Sin was still going to be a total loss.

I'm so sorry, Jax.

Sitting down in the small room's uncomfortable plastic chair, Allie's heart felt heavy as she slipped on the pair of inexpensive canvas shoes. She still couldn't believe the jerks had burned down Jax's beautiful nightclub, and her heart physically hurt for the poor man who'd been murdered, simply because he was trying to keep her and Wade safe.

It seemed like the more people tried to help her, the more those same people got hurt.

Allie sat there with her hands clenched together in her lap. She was so fucking tired of it all. Death...destruction... when was it going to end?

"Knock, knock." Wade peeked his head around the privacy curtain's edge.

His eyes were red and puffy, the skin on his forehead, cheek, and chin marred with soot. When he spoke, his voice sounded rough and scratchy, as if he'd been fighting a bad cold

"Hey." She forced a small smile. She, too, sounded like she'd been huffing and puffing on six packs of cigarettes.

Not that Allie would know. She'd never smoked before, but it was the best way she knew to describe the effects the smoke had on their bodies.

"I hear you're good to go." He squatted down next to her.

"I am." She nodded, and then took in the plain gray hoodie, jeans, and boots he was wearing. "I see Maggie brought you some clean clothes, too?"

"She did."

Allie reached for his hand and held it in her lap. "You have really good friends here, Wade."

"They're your friends now, too."

Feeling incredibly emotional, she had to fight back tears. "What are we going to do?" she whispered, desperate for the answer that would bring all this madness to an end.

"We're going to keep going, one day at a time, until we find these bastards and end them."

End them. Allie didn't ask for clarification, because frankly, she didn't care.

It didn't matter to her whether the men responsible for all that had happened were put behind bars or into the ground. Right or wrong, she'd probably be more relieved if Costa and his men were killed, but only so she could go on with her life without fear of something like this ever happening again.

And what kind of person did that make her?

"Hey." Wade's deep voice tore through her disconcerting thoughts. "Look at me."

Allie lifted her hesitant gaze to his, fearful he could tell what she'd just been thinking.

"We're going to find Costa, and we will bring him down."

"But how many more people have to die before that happens?"

Tears flooded her then. Tears of fear and sorrow. Guilt and regret. And the sweet man kneeling before her didn't try to fix it or explain it all away.

He simply lifted her into his arms, sat down in that Godawful chair, and held her until the river of emotions finally ran dry.

When her emotional breakdown was over, Wade continued to hold her a little longer before he spoke up again. "My boss wants us to stay at the office until this thing blows over."

Frowning, Allie drew in a stuttering breath. "The FBI office? Is there even a place for us to sleep there?"

"There is, actually." He nodded. "Up on the top floor, there are a handful of rooms with beds and his and hers locker rooms to shower. They use them for when agents from other divisions come for the different training courses we hold each year. Right now, they're between sessions, so the rooms are all empty."

Allie thought about it and realized there really wasn't a better option. Like they'd decided before, a hotel would leave them too vulnerable. Wade's building, however, was about as secure a place as they could find.

No one would be allowed past the main entrance without proper I.D. Plus, it was the freaking FBI. It's not like Costa or his men were going to waltz right through the front door.

"Twin beds, huh?" Her lips curved into a half-smile. "I guess that would work. It'll be like summer camp."

Wade's laughter reverberated through her. "Summer camp. I like it. Although, I do have to warn you...I may sneak into your bed in the middle of the night."

The image of the two of them trying to fit together in a twin-sized bed was more than a little amusing. Giving him her first real smile since the fire, Allie said, "You'd better."

THE NEXT MORNING, SHE AND WADE WERE DOWNSTAIRS WITH his and Noah's unit. Together, they'd gone through the footage from the traffic cameras mounted along the street where Jax's club was located. It was already dark outside when the fire was started, and the video quality was grainy, making it difficult to see with any sort of details.

But as the recorded images unfolded, Allie quickly realized it was more than enough.

She watched with horror as a dark SUV pulled up in front of *Sin*. A man wearing a hat, dark sweatshirt, and dark pants got out, pointed a gun at Jax's guard, and shot him without a second's hesitation.

Then he pulled something from his pocket, opened the club's front door, and tossed whatever it was inside before sliding the dead man's heavy weight against the door and walking back to the SUV. The minute his door was shut, whoever had been driving sped away.

"They executed that man simply because he was there."

"No witnesses that way." Noah looked down at her. "That's how ruthless these assholes are."

"You see the gun?" Wade posed the question to his partner.

"The suppressor?" The other man turned to him.

Wade nodded. "Explains why the guy in the back had no idea about the fire or the shooting until it was too late. The shot made very little noise, and the fire was already in full blaze before the smoke ever reached the rear exit."

Allie didn't understand. "Why leave if the point of the fire was to draw us out?"

"It wasn't." Wade explained. "Did you see how the guy moved the guard's body in front of the door before he left?"

"Yeah, but I just thought that was so people wouldn't notice him right away." She replayed that portion of the video in her head. "When we got to the door, you couldn't get it open. That's why we had to break the window." The more she talked it through, the more sense it began to make.

"He moved that man's body so we couldn't get out. Whoever that was wanted us to die in that fire, didn't they?"

"Yeah, baby." Wade's expression turned to stone. "They sure as fuck did. And even with all this"—he motioned to the big screen on the wall—"we're still no farther than we were when we started."

"Not exactly.'"

All three turned to see Wade's boss entering the open work space. His expression was guarded, and the way he was looking at Wade made Allie's nerves stand up and take notice.

"I need you to come with me," he spoke directly to Wade.

"Okay."

Allie started to go with him, but the man in charge stopped her with a raised hand. "Sorry, Miss Andrews. I need to speak to Agent Crenshaw, alone."

"Oh." She blinked awkwardly. "Of course."

Turning his head, Wade's dark gaze met hers. With a wink and a smirk she knew was meant to comfort her, he promised, "I'll be right back."

She watched as the two men left through the opened doorway and into the elevators. "Wonder what that's all about."

"Hard telling." Noah shrugged. "Hunt can be a hard man to read."

Allie thought she'd read the man just fine, and if her hunch was correct, something big was about to happen.

"I need to go through some files," Noah spoke up again. "You want me to see if Maggie's free to take a coffee break?"

A break was exactly what she needed. "Sure. Thanks."

Picking up his phone, Noah dialed his wife's extension.

A few short minutes later, Allie and Maggie were sitting at one of the indoor coffee shop's small, round tables.

They talked about the fire and Jax. Maggie assured her the former Navy SEAL would bounce back from it all better than before. They discussed the case, and what it was like sleeping in the dorm-like beds upstairs, and Maggie even shared a funny story about something Noah had done the last time they'd had a date night.

But all the while, in the back of Allie's mind, she couldn't help but wonder how big the shoe was that was waiting to drop. Because one thing was for sure...

Whatever SAC Hunt was discussing with Wade this very minute, it wasn't good.

"You're not firing me, are you?" Wade attempted to lighten his boss's foul mood. "Because I swear, I haven't done anything wrong...lately."

"Have a seat, Crenshaw." Hunt pointed to one of two chairs at the small table in the center of the room.

A room that was typically used to interrogate persons of interest.

All semblance of joking vanished. "What the hell is going on?"

"There's someone here to see you."

"Okay...." Wade let his voice trail off.

"The camera has been turned off, and I've locked the observation room next door so no one will be able to listen in on your conversation."

"Seriously, Boss. What's this about?" Wade looked at the closed door and back to the man in charge. "Does this have something to do what happened at Sin?"

"Sort of."

Sort of?

Wade opened his mouth to demand a more direct answer, when the door to the room opened, and the guest he'd been waiting on arrived.

What. The. Fuck?

The guy had a few more wrinkles around his eyes, and his dark blond hair had begun to recede, but it was a face Wade would recognize anywhere.

"Ryan?" He found himself staring back at a dead man.

"Hey, Wade." The man who'd once been his closest friend stood before him. With his left arm in a sling, he smiled and said, "Long time no see."

His eyes flew back to his boss's. "Is this some sort of joke?"

"It's no joke. As you can see, Agent Landry's alive and well. More or less. He's already given me the rundown of what happened, but I'll give you two some privacy so he can fill you in, as well."

Still stunned by Ryan's unexpected appearance, Wade couldn't formulate a response. Instead, he stood there, staring at the man he'd only just begun to mourn as his boss left the room, shutting the door behind him.

"Reynolds told me you were dead." The tone of his voice was completely deadpan.

"That's because he thinks I am." Ryan took a step toward him. "In fact, the only people who know I'm still alive are you and Hunt."

Wade felt gutshot and confused as fuck. "What the hell happened?"

"Two nights ago, I got home from work to find a man standing in my living room. I pulled my weapon, got a shot off, but the asshole ducked and rolled, so I missed. He fired as I dove behind my couch at the last second. Next chance I had, I decided to take it. Unfortunately, he was faster." Ryan shrugged his bad shoulder.

"But your car...Reynolds said they found it in the water."

"When I was hit, I blacked out. The dipshit who was sent to kill me thought I was dead." The man snorted. "Lucky for me, he didn't bother checking for a pulse."

"How'd you get away?"

"I came to as the shooter and a man I'm assuming was his partner were putting me into the trunk of my car. Figured my best chance to get away was to play dead."

"You could've drowned, you realize that, right?"

"Calculated risk." Ryan spoke about his own almost-murder as if it were just another day at the office. "As soon as the water got to my face, I held my breath and waited for the car to hit the bottom. Knew the pressure would be equalized out by then, so I used the emergency latch in my trunk and swam to the surface. Caught air just as the sons of bitches were driving away."

"Jesus." Wade shook his head. "You're lucky they didn't see you."

The guy's mouth curved up into his infamous smirk. "Luck's my middle name, apparently."

Walking over to the table, Wade plopped his ass in one of the chairs. "They came after Allie and I last night." He ran a hand down his face. "Burned down the place where we were staying. Executed the guy keeping guard."

"Another agent?"

He shook his head. "Friend of a friend."

As if he didn't think this situation could get any weirder, he'd just referred to Jax Monroe as a friend.

"Glad you made it out, brother."

Wade nodded absentmindedly. "The thing I don't get is, how did they find us?"

"It's Costa." Ryan sat in the other chair. "How the hell does he do anything and get away with it?"

"Yeah, but this is more than that. I mean, how did they even know Allie was here in Denver?" He studied his former partner closely. "Other than my unit and two guys I'd trust with my life, *you* were the only person I told."

Okay, so apparently Jax had graduated to that kind of friend.

Whatthefuckever.

"Me?" The other man's spine stiffened. With a scowl, he shot daggers out of his eyes. "You think *I'm* the one who ratted you out to Costa? Dude, are you out of your fucking mind?"

Ryan shot out of his chair so fast, the damn thing toppled backward.

Wade also stood. "Who else, then, Ryan? You're the *only* one from D.C. who knew Allie was here with me! If it wasn't you, then who?"

"Fuck you, Crenshaw!" Ryan spoke between a set of clenched teeth. "They came after me, too, remember? You don't believe me?"

With harsh, angry movements, he removed his sling and tossed it onto the floor. Using his good hand, he stretched the collar of his t-shirt revealing a white padded bandage with a dark crimson stain in the middle. Peeling back one corner, Ryan grimaced as he revealed the fresh wound.

It was definitely a gunshot wound. A recent one, at that. The hole had been crudely stitched together, the puckered skin around it red and angry.

Shit.

Wade didn't know if he was relieved or disappointed. No,

he didn't want to think his former partner was dirty, but at the same time, if it was Ryan who'd sold them out to Costa, at least they'd have *something* to work with.

"Satisfied?" Ryan pressed the bandage back into place and picked up his sling.

"Sorry, man. This whole case has me turned upside down."

And the only thing keeping him grounded through it all was Allie.

"Look, I get it, all right? Trust me, I'm as pissed off about all this shit as you are."

Wade doubted that. "Someone in the D.C. unit has to be in Costa's pockets. It's the only thing that makes since."

"I'm not arguing that. All I'm doing is trying to convince the guy who used to be like my brother that it isn't *me*."

"All right." Wade agreed. "Then if not you, who?"

"I don't know. I have my theories, but it's all I've got."

"Well, it's more than we have, so let's hear them."

"It's only one, really." Ryan shook his head in disgust. "I think it might be one of our tech guys. He's been acting a little shady ever since Costa escaped."

"Anyone I know?"

His former partner shook his head again. "Guy came on board about six months after you left."

So six months after Costa was handed a life sentence. It was a stretch, but there could be something there.

"That's the thing. On paper, the guy's squeaky clean. His financials are in order, there aren't any hidden accounts or secret properties associated with him or his wife…nothing."

"Well, if he's anything like the tech analysts we have here, he'd know how to cover that shit up."

"Exactly. Which is why all I have is a fucking theory."

"You ever question him?"

"Didn't want to in case it was him. Couldn't risk spooking him, you know?"

Unfortunately, Wade did.

"All right, we need to take this out to my partner. Maybe between the three of us, we can find some sort of lead."

Because time was running out. For Allie and for him. Wade could feel it deep in his gut.

There was something else that was bugging him. "Why come here?"

Ryan's light brown brows turned inward. "What do you mean?"

"I mean, how did you know Hunt wouldn't call your boss the second you went to him?"

"I didn't." He shrugged. "Not really. But all the times you and I have talked since you left, you've always said your boss was a stand-up guy. I called him up, explained my theory to him, and he agreed to meet with me. After about fifteen minutes of hard-assed grilling, he gave me his word, he wouldn't blow my cover until after Costa was back off the streets."

Like he'd always said, SAC Hunt was a stand-up guy.

"All right, man. Let's go introduce you to my partner. I also want to put my tech guy onto yours. If there's anyone who can find a rat in the barn, it's gonna be him."

"Sounds like a plan to me." Ryan opened the door, but stopped before walking into the hall. Turning, he looked as serious as Wade had ever seen him when he said, "I'd die before turning on you. I hope you know that."

"I do." Wade slapped him on his good shoulder.

Finding Noah at his desk, Wade glanced around for Allie.

Before he could ask, Noah said, "She and Maggie are downstairs getting coffee. Don't worry...I told them both to come straight here when they were done, and I've been checking in with Maggie every five minutes."

"Good." He blew out a breath. He wasn't too concerned about Costa or his men showing their faces anywhere near here, but you never knew.

After a quick introduction, Wade went through the series of events that led Ryan to give Hunt a call. He then filled Noah in on Ryan's theory, and had Agent Wright come down so Ryan could give the tech genius the information needed to begin a deep search of the D.C. tech.

"I fucking hate this." Wade shook his head and turned to Ryan. "I know they found Allie because of an inside job. The problem is, it could be anyone in your unit. Hell, for all we know, it could be Reynolds, himself."

"No." Ryan adamantly denied the claim. "No fucking way. You worked under that man for years, Wade. You know he's as tight as they come."

Yeah, he did. But damn it, it had to be *someone* there. But who?

An idea struck. To Noah, Wade asked, "You still got that file Hunt gave you?"

"The copy of the original Costa case?" Noah picked the thick folder up from his desktop. "Got it right here. Why, what are you thinking?"

"I'm thinking we need to start at the beginning."

Ryan frowned. "What do you mean?"

Grabbing the file from Noah's hand, Wade held it up and said, "I mean, we start with this. We go through every picture and page in here. Start digging into the lives of every suspect and witness on these pages. And while we're doing that, we get the tech team down here to start doing a deep dive into every member your unit. Past and present."

"That's going to take some time," Ryan didn't sound excited at the prospect.

"There someplace else you gotta be? I mean, you're dead, right? And Allie and I sure as hell aren't going anywhere anytime soon. I say we use the time and resources we have right here to figure this shit out, once and for all."

"He's right." His current partner looked to his former. "We find the bastard who's been slipping Costa information on Wade and Allie, we might just be able to convince them to tell us where Costa is."

Wade watched and waited, praying Ryan didn't fight him on this. Not that it would matter if he did.

Up to now, they'd been reacting to everything Costa's men were dishing out. It was high time they put that shit aside and started *acting*.

Because Wade was sick and tired of spending every second of the day terrified of what was coming next. Not for himself. He could handle whatever bullshit Costa wanted to throw at him. But Allie?

He couldn't lose her. Not now. Not when they were finally starting to plan for the future.

13

"They've been at it this for days." Allie sipped on her iced Americana while Maggie nursed her hot espresso-based concoction.

It had been three days since Wade's former partner had shocked them all by showing up. Allie was so surprised when Wade introduced her to the man everyone thought was dead, that for the first time in her life, she'd found herself speechless.

The more she was around him, the more she came to realize why he and Wade had gotten along so well as partners. They were both funny and sweet, two quick-witted, smartass peas in a pod.

And they were both incredibly passionate about their jobs.

"Tell me about it." Maggie's response to her comment brought Allie back to the present. "Noah and I have stayed here so late, we've considered bunking upstairs with you guys."

"Oh, you totally should!" Allie grinned. "It would be like one big slumber party!"

"I am so glad you said slumber party, because if you'd said orgy, our new friendship would've come to a very quick end."

Coffee dripped down Allie's chin as she tried not to spit the entire mouthful out onto the table. Grabbing a napkin, she and Maggie laughed as she dried the caffeinated beverage from her skin.

"Oh, my God. I can't believe you just said that."

"What?" Maggie chuckled. "Like that's not exactly what Wade would've been thinking if he were here."

Allie considered this before nodded. "You're right. That's exactly something he would've said."

The two women were still laughing when Ryan appeared beside their table.

"Hey, Ryan." She greeted him with a smile. "You need to recharge your batteries, too?"

From across the table, Maggie snickered, and somehow Allie knew it was because she'd said the word 'batteries'.

Give the woman some coffee, and it's like she becomes a whole new person.

"Actually, I came to see you."

"Me? Why me?"

"Wade sent me to escort you back upstairs. Said he found something when he was going through Costa's old case file that he thought you should see. Something about your parents."

"Oh." Her moment of immature bliss came to an end. "Um...sure. Of course." Looking at Maggie, Allie apologized as she stood. "I'm sorry."

"Don't be." The other woman stood and grabbed her apple red blazer from the back of the chair. "It sounds important. Besides, I've got three autopsies waiting for me downstairs."

"Sounds like fun," Ryan teased.

"I wouldn't call it fun...but it's definitely interesting. You could come down and observe one, if you'd like."

"Thanks, Doc." The man started to turn green. "But I think I'll pass."

"Okay, but you're really missing out."

"I'll take your word for it."

With a soft chuckle, Maggie gave Allie a quick hug, grabbed her coffee, and headed for the stairs leading to the building's lowest level."

"Shall we?" Ryan motioned toward the main lobby.

Following him into the elevator, Allie started to push the button for the second floor when he leaned forward and pressed a different floor. "Actually, they're up on four."

"Four?" She frowned. "What's on four?"

"There's a big conference room up there. They thought it would be easier to have a larger table to spread all the documents and other stuff out in front of them."

"Oh." She supposed that made sense.

They rode the rest of the way in silence. The car stopped and the doors opened, but as Allie stepped outside the elevator, she immediately realized something wasn't right.

The fourth floor appeared to be in the beginning stages of being remodeled. The walls had been stripped to the studs, tools were scattered about, and and there was clear plastic hanging in nearly every new office space.

"Uh...I think you got the floors mixed up." She turned to get back into the elevator, but stopped short when she saw that Ryan—the man Wade considered one of his very best friends—was holding a gun.

And it was pointed directly at her.

Her heart stopped beating and her lungs froze with fear. "Ryan? Wha...what are you doing?"

"Only what I've been trying to do for the last week."

What he'd been...Oh, my God. "It was you." She stared back at him with new eyes. "All this time, you were the one leaking information to Lorenzo Costa."

He made a clicking sound with his tongue. "And they say blondes are dumb. Not you, though." Ryan smirked. "No, you are much too smart for your own good."

Allie's mind raced as she tried to think of something —*anything*—she could say to talk him out of shooting her.

"Wade's going to be looking for me," she blurted desperately. "H-he's probably scouring the place trying to find me this very second."

"Let him. By the time he puts it all together, you and I will be long gone."

So he wasn't planning on killing her here, after all. That was a good thing, right?

Oh, sure. The guy's probably going to drive you to some remote field somewhere and shoot you in the head, so the entire Denver FBI doesn't hear the gunshot. That's freaking fantastic!

Her sarcastic subconscious wasn't helping. But neither would panicking.

"What about the construction crew?" She began grasping at straws. "They could come back here any minute."

"They left for their lunch break ten minutes before I brought you up here. And today's a crew member's birthday, so they're going to a restaurant across town to celebrate. They won't be back for a couple hours."

"How do you..."

With the hand not holding the gun, Ryan pointed to himself. "Nice guy, charming personality... People like me." He looked positively smug. "Sometimes they tell me things without even realizing it."

Jesus. The man showed absolutely no remorse for what he'd done. For what he was *about* to do.

Allie was stunned into silence. She was alone with a dirty agent responsible for the murders of who knows how many people, and now he was planning to add her to the list.

She remembered how upset Wade had been when he'd heard the news of Ryan's supposed death. Her heart broke for him then, just as it did now. Because when Wade discovered the truth about his so-called friend, it would be like losing him all over again.

Focus, Al. You need to focus!

No. She needed to run.

With the hope that Ryan was serious about taking her elsewhere before ending her life, Allie spun on her heels and sprinted down the empty hallway. Behind her, she heard a low curse followed by heavy footfalls.

But she refused to stop.

Weaving around and jumping over things like heavy floor saws, tools, and scattered scraps of wood, Allie had no idea where she was going. Only that she needed to get as far away from Ryan as she could.

Panic set in when she neared the end of the long hallway. But then she saw that it branched off to the right, leading into *another* hall. One with a door that could potentially lead her to freedom.

She pushed herself forward, her leg muscles burning from the intense motion. A memory flashed through her mind of that night at the diner.

Her running to Rick's office. Pushing herself out the window. Racing down that dark alleyway and nearly getting hit by the cop car.

The next image was one that threatened to break her. It

was the first time she laid eyes on Wade. As Allie continued running, she remembered his confident yet comforting stature as he'd questioned her about what she'd seen.

She also remembered how—even in the midst of one of the worst nights of her life—she'd been struck by how strong and handsome she'd thought he was. And how, despite the fact that they'd only just met, she'd immediately felt safe in his presence.

Allie blinked, realizing she was almost to that door. Sparing a quick glance over her shoulder, she nearly screamed when she saw Ryan catching up to her.

She ran the remaining few feet. She reached for the door's metal knob. It was locked.

No!

Her pulse raced to the point she thought her heart might give out. Knowing it was her only option, she turned to the right, intending to make a run for it through the unfinished office to her left.

But Ryan was already there.

He shoved her up against the useless door. With the barrel of his gun pressed beneath her chin, he said, "Gotta give you points for tryin'. But you really should've saved your energy."

"Go to hell."

"Oh, I'm sure I will." He spun her around and pulled her hands behind her back. "But first, I have a delivery to make, and a paycheck to collect."

The clinking of metal was the only warning she had before Ryan roughly bound her wrists with a set of handcuffs.

"So that's what this all about?" Allie asked as he turned her back around. "Money?"

Ryan almost looked disappointed in her. "Don't be so

naïve. Of course, it's about money. After all, that's what makes the world go 'round."

No, that was love. And she'd finally found it with Wade, but now...

"Where are you taking me?" Allie tried—and failed—to pull her wrists free.

"To meet my boss. Oh wait, that's right. You two have already met."

He was taking her to see Costa? A rush of nausea struck with a vengeance.

She remembered what they'd done to John. Not the specifics, of course, because Wade had protected her from that horrific knowledge.

The same way he'd always protected her. God, how Allie wished he was here to do so now.

"Come on." Ryan wrapped a meaty hand around her upper arm and yanked her away from the door. With the gun pushed roughly against her ribs, he said, "If I deliver you early, there might just be a bonus in my future."

"This isn't going to work." She had no choice but to go with him. "You can't just waltz through the lobby and take me out the front doors. People will see you. They'll know what you're trying to do."

"Guess it's a good thing we aren't going out the front."

Allie's thoughts whirled as she tried to figure out how he planned on kidnapping her from a federal building. Sensing her struggle, Ryan explained his plan in perfect detail.

"See that door down there?" His gaze was focused on a door at the other end of the hall that was identical to the one she'd just tried to flee through. "That's the door the construction crew use to come and go during the day. And guess what?" He leaned in closer, his hot breath hitting her skin as he whispered into her ear. "That one *is* unlocked."

Of course, it was.

Her chin quivered, but she fought against it and held back her tears. Crying wasn't going to help, but damn if she knew what would.

"Here's what we're going to do." Ryan straightened himself back up. "Are you listening? Because I'd really hate for you to hurt yourself as we're leaving." The man was certifiable. "Just outside that door is a temporary set of metal stairs. Think of it as a makeshift fire escape. You're familiar with those, aren't you?"

At first, she didn't know what he was going on about, and then it hit her. He was talking about the way she'd escaped those men in Salado.

"You and I are going to carefully go down those stairs," He continued. "Parked at the bottom is a black SUV with federal plates. You and I are going to get in that vehicle, and then we're going to drive away."

"You stole a government vehicle?"

"All the shit I've done, and that's what you're worried about?" Ryan laughed. "You really shouldn't, though. I disabled the tracking device the department places on all the vehicles."

Oh, great. That's just...great.

"Why don't you just shoot me know and get it over with?" Allie's anger began to overshadow her fear.

"Because..." Ryan opened the door leading to the outside. "That's not what my boss wants me to do. And if I want to get paid, I have to do things his way. Exactly."

The cool fresh air should've felt comforting, but given the situation, it was just another sign of how much farther away from Wade she was getting.

"Please." Allie looked down at the series of industrial stairs. "*Please*, don't do this."

"Ah, sweetheart. It's already done."

With a somewhat gentle push, Allie had no choice but to walk down those stairs. Step by dreaded step, she marched herself to certain death. She frantically searched the area behind the building in hopes that *someone* would be there and see what was happening.

But the entire area had been blocked off with the construction crew's temporary gates, and just like Ryan had claimed, they were nowhere to be seen.

Once again on solid ground, he grabbed her arm in a bruising grip and forced her toward his getaway vehicle. Despite her efforts against it, the fear icing Allie's veins took control.

If I get in that car, I'll never see Wade again.

"No!" She began to fight. It wasn't easy, given that her hands were cuffed behind her back, but that didn't stop her from trying.

"Come on, now, Allison." Ryan's hold never wavered. "I told you before, you need to save your energy. Trust me, you're gonna need it."

Ignoring the mad man, she twisted and pulled in an attempt to break free. Shoving and kicking him as best she could, the sole of her shoe struck him in the shin. Ryan cursed and then threw her up against the SUV's back driver's side door.

Allie grunted as the back of her head smacked against the tinted window.

"Knock it off!" he yelled.

It was the first time since he'd abducted her that the man had showed any semblance of real emotion.

"I won't go with you," she hissed. "I won't!"

The blond-haired man chuckled. "It's cute that you think you have a choice."

A loud, evenly-spaced alarm began to blare from somewhere inside the building.

Looking back at the place where she should've been safe, Allie smiled. "They're coming for you, Ryan. They're going to catch you, and when they do, Wade is going to kill you for what you've done."

Of that, she had no doubt.

"Wade will have his own problems to deal with." Ryan shoved her aside and opened the passenger door. "Now get in the fucking car."

Allie locked her jaw shut and shook her head. This man may be determined to deliver her to her executioner, but she damn sure didn't have to make it easy for him.

Given the piercing alarms, she knew Wade was coming for her. If she could just buy herself enough time, he might just figure out where they are before Ryan could take her away.

"Allison..." His tone mimicked that of a frustrated parent as he pointed the gun directly at her head. "Get into the car. Now."

Though she was terrified beyond measure, Allie kept her composure and jutted her chin. Blowing out a frustrated breath, Ryan shook his head and pressed the gun's barrel against her forehead. Still, she didn't budge.

"I don't want to hurt you, but I will if I have to."

The man had a gun to her head. Did he really think he could scare her more than she already was?

"Fine." Ryan brought the weapon down to his side. "Have it your way."

Just when Allie was beginning to think he might be changing his mind, Ryan swung the gun toward her face. With her hands secured behind her back, she had no way to defend herself from the massive blow.

The gun's hard metal smacked against her left temple. Pain erupted in the side of her head, and a flash of white filled her vision. A second later, Allie's entire world went dark.

14

Fifteen minutes earlier...

"So there's nothing?" Wade looked at Agent Wright, praying he'd heard him wrong.

They'd spent the last three days looking over every inch of the original file on Lorenzo Costa. Wright and the other technical analysts had combed through every known associate of the ruthless mob boss from the time he'd started running the show up until his conviction five years earlier.

"Sorry. Most of Costa's guys are either dead or in prison, and the ones who aren't, are in the wind."

No, they were here, in Denver. Taking shots at them on fucking sidewalks and burning shit to the ground.

"What about the agents in my old unit? You find anything on them?"

"Nothing that stood out." Wright shook his head. "I mean, a few aren't sitting the best financially, but I didn't find any oddities in their deposit histories, offshore accounts, or anything like that."

"Not even the guy Ryan told us about? The one who'd been acting suspicious?"

"At first, I thought there was something there. But the further I dug, the more inconsistencies I found."

"Inconsistencies?" Wade scowled. "Like what?"

"Someone tried damn hard to make the man *appear* guilty. I won't bore you with the details, but the more I looked into it, the more I realized the suspicious activity in both his personal and professional electronic trails had been planted there. The guy's as clean as a whistle."

"Goddamn it!" Wade threw the file he'd been looking at down onto his desk.

Closing his eyes, he ran a frustrated hand through his hair. He didn't want to admit it, but he was beginning to think this bullshit was never going to end.

"There *was* something that seemed a little wonky," Wright spoke up again. "But it may be nothing."

Wade's eyes popped open. "What?" He looked at the other man with hopeful desperation.

"It has to do with a witness. The one who reported seeing Agent Landry's car being put into the lake that night."

Noah frowned. "What about her?"

"When I ran her name through my system, I discovered she was already in there."

"Well yeah." Wade nodded. "Because she was a witness to the disposal of a federal agent's body."

The five-six man shook his dark head. "I'm not talking about that report. I'm saying she was already in the system *before* she called to report the incident at the lake."

What the hell? "From what?"

"That's the thing. It took me a minute because her file was sealed."

"Sealed?" Wade shared a look with Noah. "Why the fuck would her file be sealed?"

"Same reason most civilian files are locked." Agent Wright stared up at Wade, waiting for him to connect the dots.

Two seconds later, he did.

"She's an informant."

The young agent nodded. "Like I said, it took me a bit, but I finally managed to bypass the security lock on the woman's file. Turns out, she's worked as a C.I. for the past four years."

"Okay, so who's the agent she signed up under?"

Wright hesitated, his brown eyes bouncing from Wade, to Noah, and back to Wade.

"Spit it out, Michael," Noah ordered. "What's the name of the agent this witness works for?"

Sympathy filled the thin man's eyes. "I'm sorry, Agent Crenshaw. The witness works for your previous partner... Agent Ryan Landry."

Wade stumbled back a step. No. No fucking way.

Ryan couldn't be the leak. He *couldn't* be.

"I saw the bullet wound, myself," he argued more with himself than anyone else. "The guy was shot and left for dead."

"Or maybe he shot himself to make it look that way."

Wade's eyes flew to Noah's. "You think Ryan risked killing himself to fake his own death? That's crazy!"

"It is. It's also smart."

"Smart?"

"Adds plausibility to his story." Noah took a step closer to him. "Listen, man. Nobody wants to think someone they know and trust is dirty, but it's the only thing in this shitshow of a case that makes sense."

Wade's mind raced to find another explanation. Something that didn't lead to the conclusion that the same man who'd had his back for years was behind the attempts on his and Allie's lives.

But the longer he stood there, the more he realized his current partner was right.

"Run him." Wade turned to Agent Wright. Now was the perfect time, because the guy had just left to go to the restroom and grab them some lunch from the food cart stationed on the floor above them. "Dig up anything and everything you can on the man. And hurry, before he gets back."

He'd originally told the guy not to worry about running Ryan's background, because he'd believed the bastard's lies. But now that he'd begun to accept that his friend was in bed with Costa, the more believable the theory became.

"I'm on it."

Rather than go back upstairs, Wright sat down at his assigned desk right there and began typing. Two minutes later, he leaned back in his chair and said, "Found it!"

Wade's heart fell, but he pushed his personal feelings aside and went over to see what the man was referring to.

"Whoever tried covering Agent Landry's tracks was good, but lucky for us, I'm better."

"What the fuck did you find, Michael?" Wade growled. He knew he was being an asshole, but they probably only had seconds before Ryan returned.

"Right. Sorry." Wright leaned up and pointed to his screen. "See these large deposits here? They were made to an account attached to a bank in Geneva."

"Switzerland?" Noah asked to be sure.

"That's the one." The brilliant man nodded. "Anyway, this same amount has been deposited once a month for the past five years."

"Wait..." Wade stopped him. "Five years? That can't be right."

If it was, that meant Ryan started working for Costa either right before or right after the man's trial. Either way...

"That son of a bitch."

"There's one more thing," Wright added begrudgingly. "I overheard Agent Landry re-telling the story of his harrowing escape to Miss Andrews the other day. He said he was able to get out of the trunk by way of the safety release inside. But I just looked up the report from when they found the car... The pictures of the trunk are clear, and show every angle. That car doesn't have a safety release."

I'm going to kill him. Slowly. With my bare hands.

"I know it's not the news you were hoping to hear." Noah put a hand on Wade's shoulder. "But at least we finally have someone to interrogate. And given your history with Landry, he may be smart enough to open up to you about where Costa's been hiding out."

"Oh, I'll get the lying bastard to talk." Wade clenched his jaw. "If I don't kill him, first."

"Speaking of which..." Agent Wright glanced toward the unit's entrance. "Shouldn't he be back by now?"

The man's words sent a rush of panic through Wade's entire system. The same terrifying realization must've struck Noah, too, because they shot each other a look at the exact same time and said, "Allie."

She and Maggie had been taking regular coffee breaks together ever since Wade and Allie had been staying upstairs. Before this moment, Wade had been grateful to Maggie for taking time out of her busy day to help give Allie a respite from everything. Plus, it was a way for the two women to get to know each other even better.

But now...

"Lock the building down!" Wade yelled to whoever was listening as he took off in a dead sprint toward the stairs.

Knowing they would be faster than waiting on an elevator, he burst through the stairwell door. Luckily, it was located near the women's restroom, just across from the elevators near their office space.

He ran down toward the main floor as fast as his feet would take him. Noah was right on his tail.

"Hey, you," Maggie's voice came through Noah's phone. "Shouldn't you be working?"

"Please tell me Allie's with you." His partner's words sounded disjointed as they continued down the stairs.

"No...I've been back in the lab for about fifteen minutes." There was a pause and then, "I thought she was with you. Agent Landry said—"

"What?" Wade demanded to know. "What did he say?"

"Noah, what's going on?"

"I'll explain later, but right now, I need you to tell me exactly what happened when you left Allie."

"O-okay...um...we were at the coffee shop, and Agent Landry came to our table. He said Wade had sent him to get Allie because you guys had found something...I think he mentioned something about her parents' case."

That motherfucker.

"Did you see where they went?"

"No, I'm sorry." Maggie's tone was full of regret. "I took the stairs, like I usually do. They were walking to the lobby elevators when I left. Is she okay? Did something happen?"

"Landry's the leak," Noah told his wife as Wade pushed

open the door to the main lobby. "He's been working for Costa this whole time."

"Oh, God, Noah. I'm so sorry. I never would've left her, if I'd known."

"I know, baby. It's not your fault. Listen, I gotta go."

"Call me the second you find her!"

"I will. I love you."

Noah ended the call while Wade frantically searched the area for the woman he loved. "They're not here." He shook his head. "She's not fucking *here!*"

"It's only been a few minutes." Noah pointed out. "They couldn't have gone far."

Pulling his own cell from his pants pocket, Wade called Agent Wright, praying the man answered on the first ring. Luckily, he did.

"You find them?"

"No." Wade swallowed the giant knot of emotion buried deep in his throat. "I need you to pull up the building's security footage. Start with the cameras on the lower level, near the coffee shop. Rewind to twenty minutes ago. You should see Landry entering the shop."

He could hear the man's fingers flying expertly across the keyboard. One long, torturous minute later, he heard, "Found him!"

"I need to know where he and Allie went once they left."

More clicking and then, "Okay, they got into the elevator. Switching to that footage, now." Over the next few seconds, Wright continued working his magic. "They went to the fourth floor."

Wade's eyes flew to Noah's. "That floor's closed for construction." He looked at his watch. *Ah, Christ.* It was lunchtime, which meant the crew had probably left.

He ran to the stairs, refusing to wait for a damn elevator to take him to where Allie might be. With Noah right behind him, he asked Agent Wright, "Are the cameras working up there?"

"They were disabled due to the remodel."

"Fuck!"

Wade pushed his body to its limits, running as fast as his legs would take him. Skipping every other step, he and Noah finally reached the fourth-floor door. Sliding his phone into his jacket pocket, Wade pulled out one of his earbuds—which automatically connected to his phone when activated—and slid it into his ear.

Weapons drawn, their training kicked in as he and his partner opened the door with caution.

His head moved on a swivel as he looked for any signs of Allie or Ryan. The place was a mess, the air rich with the smell of sawdust.

Using hand signals, he let Noah know he was headed to his right. The sound of his own blood rushed through his ears as he realized he wanted nothing more than to find her, but at the same time, he was terrified that he would.

With the space completely isolated and empty, it would be the perfect spot to leave a body and get away.

No! He shook the unthinkable notion away. Allie wasn't dead. Their connection was too strong. Too unbreakable. He'd know it if she were.

He and Noah continued their search, but every space they checked came up empty. They'd barely made it halfway through the partially-renovated floor when Wright's voice filled his ear once more.

"They left."

Wade stopped dead in his tracks. "What do you mean, they left?"

"The cameras on that floor are still down, but the ones

in the back of the building are business as usual. Seventeen minutes ago, Agent Landry and Miss Andrews exited through that floor's west exterior door. They went down the temporary fire escape and took off in one of our SUV's. Guy had it parked and ready."

Oh, God. Wade covered his mouth with his hand. Feeling more lost than ever before, he looked to his partner who was walking back in his direction. "He took her, Noah. The fucker *took* her!"

Bending at the waist, Wade rested his hands on his knees. He drew in long, slow breaths through his nose, releasing them out his mouth in an effort to control the need to vomit.

What Agent Wright had just told him finally sank in.

"Wait." He stood straight once more. "Did you say he took off in one of *our* cars?"

"Black SUV, yeah," the other agent confirmed. "Guy must've picked the lock and then hot-wired it. I was able to get the plate, so I'm running the GPS now."

Wade pulled the earbud from his ear and pulled out his phone so Noah could hear. They stood together, waiting impatiently for the guy to do his thing.

"Shit," Wright cursed. "Landry disabled the vehicle's system."

Bile rushed to the base of Wade's throat.

"Hold on...I think I've got something.'

Hope began to bloom once more. "What?"

"Give me just a second..."

Wade growled. "We don't have seconds, Michael.'

"Almost got it...there! I almost forgot about it, but all of the agencies' new vehicles have a back-up in case the GPS system goes down."

"What are you saying?" Wade thought he knew, but he needed to be sure.

"I'm saying, I was able to bypass the GPS breach. I know where they are, Wade! I'm sending you the link to the system now, so you can follow them."

Tears of relief threatened to fall, but Wade forced them away. This wasn't over, yet.

It wouldn't be over until Landry, Costa, and every other fucker who'd dared tried to take what was his had been dealt with, and Allie was back in his arms, where she belonged.

I'll find you, baby. Please hold on a little longer. I'm coming for you!

15

ALLIE SAT in the wooden chair and tried with all her might not to give up. It was hard, given her current situation, but those alarms she'd heard had given her hope.

Something she'd begun to think she'd never feel again.

Her head pounded from where Ryan had pistol-whipped her, and there was sticky, drying blood matted in her hair and on her head and cheek.

She'd regained consciousness a few minutes ago, her heart sinking when she found that her wrists were still cuffed behind her, and her ankles were tied to the chair's legs with plastic ties.

So far, no one had come into the dark, dank room they'd put her in. Which wasn't necessarily a bad thing.

If they weren't in here, they weren't torturing her. And the longer they stayed away, the better the odds that someone would find her.

Wade.

Allie pictured his handsome face. By now, he had to know she'd gone missing, and that his former partner and friend was the one responsible.

Her eyes closed, her heart shattering into a million pieces for how worried he must be. He must be frantic, but she knew he was out there somewhere, looking for her.

Ryan disabled the GPS, remember? There's no way for them to track your location.

Hell, *she* didn't even know where she was. Still, Allie refused to give up hope. After all, it was the only thing she had left.

Men's voices reached her from the other side of the door. Her breathing picked up and the fear she continued to fight coursed through her veins as Ryan entered the decrepit room, followed by Lorenzo Costa.

Tony Antonelli and Vinnie Markell—the two men he'd sent to her apartment in Salado—fell in line behind them. Their presence most likely meant to intimidate her even more than she already was.

Good luck with that, fellas!

"Miss Andrews, we meet again." Costa walked toward her.

He was dressed in a gray suit, white button-up, and flowered tie. Apparently, even being a fugitive from justice didn't put a damper on the man's style.

Allie chose to remain silent, mainly because nothing she had to say to this man would do her any good.

"You're a hard woman to kill." Costa smiled. "I must say, I'm surprised at what a resourceful challenge you've become."

Still, she said nothing.

"You know, Allison... May I call you Allison? It's very impolite to ignore someone when they are speaking to you."

When Allie continued with her refusal to hold a conversation with the twisted bastard, Costa motioned to Vinnie, the man who'd shot her once before. With a smug look on his mean little face, the short asshole marched right over and backhanded her as hard as he could.

She cried out, the blow sending the chair toppling to the side. But before she could fall to the ground, Vinnie pulled her upright, slamming it back down on all fours.

The pain in her right jaw exploded throughout the entire right side of her face. The headache she already had intensified to the point Allie's eyes began to water, and the metallic taste of fresh blood coated the tip of her tongue.

"Let's try this again, shall we?" Costa spoke calmly. "I'm going to ask you a question. You will answer honestly. Ready?"

"Fuck you."

The aging mob boss laughed. "That's a start, hey boys?" Turning his expression ice cold, Costa asked her, "What does the FBI know?"

Allie considered the question before answering. "They know you're a murdering son of a bitch." She glanced at Vinnie and then Tony. "They know who you are, and that you're the ones who ambushed me at my apartment in Texas." Then, to Ryan, Allie said, "And by now, Wade knows what a piece of shit partner you really were."

"Ask for an honest answer, you get an honest answer." Costa smiled. "What I meant, Miss Andrews, was do they know where I am?"

"They will." She truly did believe that. "They're going to find you, and when they do, they're going to kill you all."

"So that's a no." Costa appeared pleased. "Good. That means we have some time, you and I."

"Time for what?"

"Time for you to see what happens to young women who stick their noses where they don't belong."

Allie felt like she was going to throw up, but she didn't

dare let this man see her fear. "You going to torture me like you did John Napier?"

"Ah, Marshal Napier. A strong one, that man. Did you know, he actually refused to give your location? At first, anyway. But then Tony, here, started cutting off his fingers, and by the time he got to the last tiny pinky, the man simply couldn't resist any longer."

Bile filled her throat, making her physically gag. She'd known the man had been put through hell, but they'd cut off John's *fingers* to make him talk?

Oh, John. I'm so, so sorry!

"Don't worry." Costa smiled at her as if they were friends. "We're not going to do that to you. After all, men in my line of work do follow a certain number of rules. One of those being, no torturing women."

"But attempted murder and kidnapping is okay?"

The man laughed. "You know, if you hadn't been the one responsible for putting me in prison, I might actually like you."

The thought nearly left her gagging once more.

"So if torture isn't on the agenda, what is?"

"To start? I thought I'd let Tony, here, take you for a spin." The tall man standing behind him smiled with a sickening grin. "He's fancied you ever since you gave him and Vinnie the slip back in Texas. And since he's been such a loyal employee, I figured he's earned it. Don't you?"

Tony was going to *rape* her? She'd rather die than endure something like that.

"You don't have to do this." Allie pleaded with the man in charge. "You broke free, you can go anywhere you want. Please, just leave me here and go." The panic she'd tried so hard to keep at bay broke through. "Just leave me here and *go!*"

"Costa, man." Ryan looked over at his boss. "She's right. Let's just leave her here and get the hell out before the Feds figure out where we are."

"You said they couldn't track you," Vinnie spoke up. "Said you disabled the GPS or whatever."

Ryan nodded. "I did. Stopped and tossed the plates as soon as we were out of eyeshot from the Bureau, too. But Crenshaw...my former partner? He's the best I've ever worked with. He's also her lover." He tilted his head in her direction. "Trust me, we don't want to be here if that guy shows up."

"What the fuck, Landry?" Tony charged toward him. "What kind of bullshit you trying to pull? You getting soft on us?"

"Yeah, Landry." Vinnie fed off the other's guy's comments. "Maybe you've grown sweet on our girl here."

I'm not your girl, asshole.

Allie remained quiet as she watched the heated exchange. If they were arguing with each other, then maybe they'd forget about her and move on.

"I'm not fucking sweet on her, assholes!" Ryan yelled. "I'm just trying to keep our asses alive."

"Well, maybe we don't need you alive anymore." Tony pulled his weapon and pointed it at Ryan's head.

"Dude, what the fuck?" Ryan shot Costa a look. "Are you seeing this shit?"

"I do." Costa nodded. "And I'm beginning to wonder if Vinnie is right. Are you and Miss Andrews involved?"

"The fuck? I just told you, she's Crenshaw's girl!"

"Yeah, but you've been hanging out with them an awful lot lately," Tony challenged.

Clearly pissed, Ryan looked at Costa. "To get to her, so I could bring her to *you!* Which I did." Drawing in a breath, he said, "You know what? Y'all can do whatever you want to her. Just pay me what I'm owed, and I'll get out of your hair."

"You leave, when I say you leave." Costa's tone was calm and controlled.

"Jesus, man. This shit's getting out of control."

Tony moved closer to Ryan, his gun still trained on the crooked agent. "You know what I think? I think *you're* the one who's out of control."

"Yeah? Then shoot me, asshole. Or don't you have the balls?"

Tony's expression hardened and his finger began to tighten around the trigger. Just when Allie thought she was going to witness Ryan's murder—his *real* murder—the trained man flung his wounded arm up. In an impressive defensive move, Ryan swung that same arm around, using the other hand to disarm Tony. Then he raised the weapon and fired a bullet square between the tall man's eyes.

Tony dropped where he stood, the look of shock still on his face as his lifeless body landed.

"What the fuck!" Vinnie stared down at his partner with horror.

Ryan turned the gun on him. "One more word, and you'll be right beside him on the fucking floor."

Oh, God, oh, God, oh, God!

"See, Vinnie?" Costa didn't appear to be affected by the sudden murder that had just taken place less than two feet from where he stood. "*That* is how you take care of business."

Vinnie turned his beady eyes in her direction. "So what are we going to do about her?"

Allie had just seen Ryan shoot a man in cold blood. A very, very bad man, but still. No way would he let her walk away after that.

"Not much else we can do." Ryan faced her. "If it makes you feel any better, I really was starting to like you. It's no wonder Wade loves you so much."

He lifted the gun, its barrel pointed straight at her head.

"No, Ryan!" Allie begged. "Please, God. Please, don't do this! *Please!*"

"Sorry, Allie. It's nothing personal."

With tears running down her cheeks, Allie squeezed her eyes shut and waited for the end to come. Using her last seconds on this earth, she brought back her favorite memories with Wade.

The day they met. Sitting on the couch in that very first safe house, laughing at Spaceballs and other silly movies. Making love in his apartment. Him hauling her into that room at Sin where he kissed her like mad and confessed his love.

Him asking her to marry him beneath the falling water in Jax's shower.

Those were the memories she wanted to take with her when she left this world for whatever was on the other side.

I love you, Wade. I'll always love you.

Allie heard a loud *bang*. She waited for the pain to hit, but it never did. But maybe that was how it was supposed to be. Maybe, in the moment of death, there was no pain.

There was another sound. The scrambling of feet and Ryan's and Vinnie's panicked voices. That wasn't right. If she was dead, she shouldn't be able to hear...

Allie opened her eyes right as Ryan came behind her and put his gun to her temple.

What the...

In the very next moment, Wade burst through the door. He didn't so much as blink before he pulled his trigger, killing Vinnie instantly. At the same time, Costa reached for his weapon, but the man wasn't quite fast enough.

Noah's bullet caught him in the chest, right in the center of the bastard's cold and empty heart. Both men fell to the ground, their open eyes staring into nothing.

Their souls already burning in hell.

Allie couldn't believe her eyes. Wade had found her. He'd *found* her!

But there was still one problem left, and that man was still standing behind her. His gun still pressed painfully against her head.

"Drop the weapon, Landry," Wade ordered.

"Sorry, brother. No can do."

"You and I both know how this ends if you don't."

"Actually, I don't know that. Way I see it, I have the upper hand." He pushed that damn gun even harder against her temple.

Allie stared at Wade. She couldn't take her eyes off him.

His taut arms were nearly trembling with his apparent efforts to keep from shooting the man who'd once been his friend. The muscles in his forearms flexed, the veins there bulging.

But all Allie could think of was at least she got to see him one last time before she died.

"You've got two choices, Ryan," Wade spoke up again. "You leave here walking or in a body bag. You decide."

"You always were an arrogant prick." Ryan pulled a knife from his pocket and flipped the blade open. Keeping his gun trained on her and his eyes on Wade, he squatted down and cut the ties at her ankles loose. "Get up," he ordered, yanking her to her feet with a hand beneath her right arm.

Allie's legs shook beneath her to the point she wasn't sure she could even walk. Sliding the knife back into his pocket, Ryan wrapped his free arm around her neck from behind and he began to move.

"Drop your guns or watch her die. *You* decide," Ryan mocked Wade.

"You kill her, you lose the only leverage you have."

"Maybe. But at least I'd have the pleasure of knowing you had to watch her bleed out right in front of you."

The man's macabre statement had Wade flinching. For the first time since entering the room, his gaze slid to hers.

"I'm sorry," Allie told him.

She knew it wasn't really her fault, but she never wanted to put him in the position to have to choose between her life and taking another's. Especially someone he knew and, at one time, loved.

"Nothing to be sorry for, sweetheart." Wade looked back at her with more love than she deserved. "It's going to be okay, you hear me?"

Ryan chimed back in with, "Don't lie to the poor girl."

Wade looked back at his former partner with disgust. "What happened to you?" His brows furrowed. "You were one of us. Fighting to take men like these off the fucking street."

"What happened?" Ryan spat back. "You left me, that's what happened. You left, and everything went to shit."

"Bullshit!" Wade held his gun steady. "I know you were already on Costa's payroll before I left."

"Yeah, well maybe I was. But come on, man. You know what it's like. We're out there day after day, risking our asses, and for what? A few bucks in the bank and a half-assed pension and shiny gold watch when we retire?"

"Seriously? Jesus, man." Wade shook his head. "No one goes into the FBI to get rich. You know that shit when you signed up."

"Yeah, well that was before I made some poor investments and lost my entire life's saving."

"So you go to work for scum like this?"

"Pays the bills a hell of a lot better than Uncle Sam. Besides, you were always the department's Golden Boy. When you left, they stuck me with some schmuck from Idaho who couldn't find his own ass if he had to. The job…it wasn't the same after you left."

Wade scowled. "So now this is *my* fault? Are you even listening to yourself right now?"

"I don't expect you to understand." Ryan shifted his arm higher, making it harder for her to breathe. "And none of this BS matters anyway. What does matter is your girl's got about ten seconds to live if you don't put your fucking guns away and walk the fuck out of here. Come on, brother. You know I'll do it."

"Wade?" Allie choked out his name.

His gray eyes turned back to hers. His stare was so deep, so intense, she could've sworn it could reach the very depths of her soul.

"Do you trust me, sweetheart?" He asked softly.

Allie did her best to nod. "Yes."

"Good."

Everything seemed to stop around her, the next seconds happening in super slow motion.

Wade blinked once. His expression turned deadly, and his trained gaze moved back to the man standing half-behind, and half-beside her.

Allie saw his chest fall with a slow, controlled exhale. A fraction of a second later, his finger squeezed his trigger.

Wade's bullet struck Ryan. His body jerked, the gun in his hand falling to the ground seconds before his body followed.

The next thing she knew, she was in Wade's arms. The danger was finally over.

Though she couldn't hear for the ringing in her ear, she could tell Wade was yelling her name, running his hands up and down her body and asking if she was okay. She nodded, then looked down at Ryan, who was lying in a fast-growing pool of his own blood.

Wade's bullet had hit him on the right side of his throat, severing the carotid artery on impact. The man had seconds left to live.

Allie read his lips as he sputtered his final word.

"B-broth...er." Ryan reached for Wade.

But Wade simply shook his head, his deep voice sounding muffled as he told the dying man. "I'm not your brother."

Ryan coughed once. A spray of blood and spit flying from his lips. And then...it was over.

EPILOGUE

A beach in the Bahamas...four months later...

"You may kiss the bride."

Wade barely waited for the minister to say the words before pulling Allie into his arms and kissing her as if there was no tomorrow. Because he'd lived that possibility the day she'd disappeared from the Denver FBI office building, and those hours spent not knowing where she was or if she was still alive...

They were the most agonizing moments of his entire life.

The small, intimate crowd cheered, reminding him once again that Allie was still with him. She was okay and she was here. In this moment, and for every moment moving forward.

For the rest of their lives.

Declan used his fingers to release a high-pitched whistle into the warm ocean breeze. Noah hollered out, both he and Maggie smiling wide as they looked at Wade and Allie with all the love and happiness friends should have for each other.

At first, Jax didn't think he'd be able to made the trip. But at the last minute, he'd changed his mind, deciding to take a break from putting the finishing touches on his newly rebuilt club to celebrate their nuptials.

They were all here to witness his and Allie's vows to love, cherish, and protect each other until death did them part. It warmed Wade's heart knowing they'd taken time out of their lives to share in the most important day of *his* life.

But right now, in this moment, the only person Wade he cared about was his wife...and the child growing inside her womb.

A few weeks after all the shit went down with Ryan and Costa, and he and Allie had settled back into his apartment, she'd discovered she was pregnant.

His first thought was how incredibly happy he was. Wade's second? He couldn't wait to be a father.

The third thing that had come to mind while processing the incredible news was that he was damn glad they'd already found a chunk of land for their dream house.

A house they'd already begun to build.

It didn't come as much of a shock that Allie was pregnant, considering neither of them had used protection. But that first time on his couch had sort of just happened, and after that, Wade had known there'd be no going back.

He'd decided right then that she was the one. The *only* one. He'd also known, without a sliver of doubt, that this day would eventually come. And the baby?

Well, that was just about the best news he'd ever heard.

Wade had been over the moon when Allie had told him about the baby. As had Noah and Maggie. Even Declan and Jax had offered their congragulations, once Allie felt it was safe to share. Now those four were here, with him and Allie, to celebrate their special day.

"I love you." Allie beamed as he pulled her out of the romantic dip and back onto her feet.

"I love you, too." Wade put a hand to her already-swelling belly. "Both of you."

Together, they walked barefoot through the sand and greeted their awaiting friends. As Wade looked around, he realized these were his *true* friends.

His family.

"Now that you're an old married couple, I suppose our nights of fun are over, huh?" Declan grinned as he picked up a glass of champagne from the small table next to them.

"On the contrary, Dec." Wade pulled Allie to his side. "*My* nights of fun are just beginning."

With a roll of his eyes and a groan, Declan slammed back the remainder of the sweet bubbly before setting the glass down and grabbing another.

"Easy, Declan." Allie chuckled. "You may end up passed out on the beach if you keep that up."

"With any luck, I'll wake up with a bikini-clad vixen by my side." The detective waggled his dark brows and lifted his glass. "Cheers."

The group laughed as Wade and Allie walked down toward the water's edge.

Turning back, he stood with his new bride as they watched the people who mattered most to them enjoy the simple festivities. They were talking and laughing, and Wade realized everyone who mattered in his life was right here, in this little space of heaven.

"So, Mr. Crenshaw." Allie looked up at him with a sly grin. "You want to stay down here, or shall we start the honeymoon early?"

Like that's even a question.

Linking his fingers with hers, Wade brought her hand to his mouth and kissed her there. "I'll go anywhere, Mrs. Crenshaw. As long as I'm with you."

Pre-Order Marked for Deception (Marked Book 3) Now!

Before Declan King was a detective with Denver's Major Crimes Division, he was the best undercover cop in the city. He was a chameleon, become whoever and whatever the job required to take down the bad guys. There wasn't anything he wouldn't do, if it meant getting the scum he was after off of his streets.

Including using the only woman to ever slip past his defenses to get the information he needed to take down his target...her father.

When he's ordered to go under once again, this time to take down his previous target's brother, Declan will have to decide... Will he pull the woman he secretly loves back into his web of deceit in order to make it happen, or will his lies end up costing him everything he's ever wanted?

ALSO BY ANNA BLAKELY

Marked Series

Marked For Death

Marked for Revenge

Marked for Deception

Marked for Obsession

Charlie Team Series

Kellan

Asher

Greyson

Rhys

R.I.S.C. Series

Taking a Risk, Part One

Taking a Risk, Part Two

Beautiful Risk

Intentional Risk

Unpredictable Risk

Ultimate Risk

Targeted Risk

Savage Risk

Undeniable Risk

His Greatest Risk

Bravo Team Series

Rescuing Katherine

Rescuing Gabriella

Rescuing Ellena

Rescuing Jenna

TAC-OPS Series

Garrett's Destiny

Coming Soon:

Beckett's Desire

Creed's Vow

Rafe's Future

WANT TO CONNECT WITH ANNA?

Newsletter signup (with FREE Bravo Team prequel novella!) BookHip.com/ZLMKFT
Join Anna's Reader Group: www.facebook.com/groups/blakelysbunch/
BookBub: https://www.bookbub.com/authors/anna-blakely
Amazon: amazon.com/author/annablakely
Author Page: https://www.facebook.com/annablakelyromance
Instagram: https://instagram.com/annablakely
Twitter: @ablakelyauthor
Goodreads: https://www.goodreads.com/author/show/18650841.Anna_Blakely

Printed in Great Britain
by Amazon